Eileen

*Again the
Israelites did evil in
the* LORD's *sight, so the*
LORD *handed them over to
the Philistines, who oppressed
them for forty years.
In those days a man named Manoah
from the tribe of Dan lived in the town
of Zorah. His wife was unable to become
pregnant, and they had no children.
The angel of the* LORD *appeared to
Manoah's wife and said, "Even though
you have been unable to have children,
you will soon become pregnant and give
birth to a son. So be careful; you must*

not drink wine or any other alcoholic drink nor eat
any forbidden food. You will become pregnant
and give birth to a son, and his hair must never
be cut. For he will be dedicated to God as a
Nazirite from birth. He will begin to rescue
Israel from the Philistines."

—JUDGES 13:1–5 (NLT)

Ordinary Women of the BIBLE

Ordinary Women of the BIBLE

HER SOURCE OF STRENGTH
RAYA'S STORY

JILL EILEEN SMITH

Guideposts
Danbury, Connecticut

ACKNOWLEDGMENTS

I'd like to thank Susan Downs for contacting me to consider writing one of these stories in the Ordinary Women of the Bible series. It is an honor to be asked, and I thank her for thinking of me.

Thanks also to my agent, Wendy Lawton, for always working out the details and supporting me throughout my writing career.

A special thanks to my friend Hannah Alexander for reading the first draft of this story and for putting my mind at ease that I had a story worth telling.

Always, I am grateful to God for my family—for Randy, who has walked with me for forty-three years and counting, and for our sons, daughters-in-law, and granddaughters. You are a great blessing to me.

Most of all, with every book God allows me to write, I grow more thankful to Him for the privilege and more awed by what He teaches me in the process. He is ever and always worthy of praise!

Dedication

To those who question and to those who pray,
may God give you the answers you seek.
This story is for you.

PART ONE

Raya's Song

The LORD is the strength of his people, a fortress of salvation for his anointed one. Save your people and bless your inheritance; be their shepherd and carry them forever.

 —Psalm 28:8–9 (NIV)

CHAPTER ONE

Raya tucked her long dark hair into her scarf as she walked, her heart beating fast. She'd hurried from the house too quickly, she realized with sudden annoyance, and left the water jar outside the door. This would never do. But the thought of returning to listen to Karmela one more time made her pause midstep. *Adonai, why is she such a frustration?*

"How long am I going to have to wait for the water?" Karmela's sarcasm had stung.

"I'm going now," Raya had said, turning to do just that, but she could not escape Karmela's final words.

"You know, if you got up before sunrise, we could feed our men properly so they wouldn't have to eat dried bread and cheese before they left to care for the sheep. Really, Raya, it's not like you have to do all of the preparation...."

Raya had reached her rooms and shut the door, cutting off Karmela's rant. Let her talk to herself, or perhaps Manoah's mother, Adah, would hear and stop her....

The memory still irritated her as she finished securing her unruly hair and glanced at the heavens. The urge to complain, to utter words she would never say, which she knew offended Adonai, rose within her. But she squelched the temptation to speak them. Her sister-in-law cared nothing for Adonai, yet her children grew up like olive plants around her father-in-law's table and were simply too perfect. Karmela did not flaunt them in front of her, for which Raya thanked Adonai. But her overall undesirable attitude and that subtle lift of her chin caused Raya's frustration to rise like a pot bubbling over.

Berating herself for her lapse, she turned to head back to the house for the water jar. She could not shirk her duty to gather the morning's water, lest Talia be forced to do the job both day and night. Since Karmela did most of the grinding and cooking—her choice as the first daughter-in-law of the household—it fell to Raya and Talia to draw the water and clean up after meals. That Ariel had married Karmela before his older brothers had wed seemed to have made Karmela proud of her status. She needn't have been, for despite the order of marriage, nothing changed the rights of Manoah as Baruch's firstborn.

If Karmela could simply curb her tongue as she worked, stop judging Raya for her barrenness, or making comments to Talia about the quality of her weaving, the household would know some measure of peace.

Why does she think herself better than we are, Adonai? She does, doesn't she? Or am I simply jealous because she has sons who follow Your law and I have not one child to carry on my husband's name?

She slowed her pace as she neared the house, intending to go unnoticed as she grabbed the jar and hurried toward the well. She would not risk another encounter with Karmela when dawn had barely risen. But even as she bore the thought, guilt assailed her. She should be kinder, less easily frustrated with the woman. She was family, after all.

Raya approached the rooms she shared with Manoah, grateful for this door that led outside, separate from the main rooms of the house of her in-laws. As it was, too many people and too many rooms filled the land they owned in their town of Zorah. But she wouldn't mind one more. Surely a small babe wouldn't take much space. They could fit his bed near their own at first, and Manoah could build another room for him as he grew. Just one child. She wouldn't ask for more. Just one to take away her shame…and to stop Karmela's haughty looks.

Oh, Adonai, what I wouldn't give for a child! The prayer came often as she walked alone to the well. *I wish I understood why You give sons to a woman who does not trust in You, yet I am denied.*

She sighed. There she was complaining again. She hurried to grab the jar and stalked off, angry with herself. Could she not control her own feelings for even a single morning? What was wrong with her that she was so emotional of late and easily troubled?

"Raya, wait!" She heard Talia's call and almost ignored it. But the sound of the one sister-in-law she adored made her stop. She could not be unkind, despite her inner turmoil.

Talia caught up with her and drew a steadying breath, a water jar also held atop her head. "I thought we could walk together."

"But you gather this evening. You don't need to come twice."

"Karmela asked for more, and Adah suggested I go with you. They are expecting guests tonight—at least that is what Elead told me before he left with Manoah to tend the flocks." Talia settled into step with Raya, who looked at her, assessing her. Talia was easy to talk to and her favorite of the women in Baruch's household. Frustrated or not, she suddenly welcomed the company.

"Visitors will make more work, but it will be nice to hear whatever news they bring."

"I think they are relatives from up in the hills, but Elead was not certain, and I didn't ask Adah. Of course, Karmela is running around barking orders and I didn't want to get in her way." She laughed, and Raya joined her.

"We really shouldn't tease about her," Raya said after a moment and another wave of guilt. "She does her best, and at least she enjoys doing most of the cooking."

Talia kept her eyes on the path, but she gave a slight nod. "I suppose, but you have to admit, it is good to laugh."

Raya held her tongue a moment before responding. "I know. You are right. I just would not want to be the person people laughed about. I already feel the watchful eye of Adah and I see her shake her head in disappointment that I have not borne Manoah a son. I will admit, today is not a good day for me." She swallowed, unable to say more.

Talia stopped and turned to face Raya. She placed one hand on her shoulder, the other still holding the jar atop her head. "You have done nothing wrong, Raya. You are too hard on yourself and I doubt very much that Adonai is upset with you for how you feel. If He would open your womb, He knows your feelings would change, so how can He blame you for feeling sad or frustrated with those who add to your shame?"

Raya tilted her head, scrunching her brows together. "Then you are saying I should blame Adonai for my barrenness?" She couldn't do that no matter what people said. The fault was hers. Either she had sinned or God had other reasons, but she would not blame Him. Could not fault Him. He gave life and breath and she would trust Him whether He gave her a child or not. Yet the yearning in her soul for a son did not abate, even with her determined conviction to be content with her life.

"No, I didn't mean it that way," Talia said, backtracking her words. "I would not fault God, but it does seem odd that He has not blessed you. So many women of old who were barren, the patriarchs' wives for example, all bore children who grew up to become great people. Perhaps God is going to do the same for you." She patted Raya's shoulder and then moved on toward the well.

Raya walked beside her, though her feet wanted to drag behind. Talia was wrong. Sarah, Rebekah, and Rachel were chosen…special to God. They were barren for a time but only because God had great reason and their offspring did great things. She was Raya, wife of Manoah from a tribe that wasn't even born of one of Jacob's wives, just a maidservant concubine. Dan—a tribe of such little significance, despite its connection to Rachel's maidservant.

God did not do miracles for barren women in obscure tribes like hers. And even if He did, for what purpose? What reason would He have for giving her a son now? What good could a son of hers do? She glanced heavenward, but the clouds scudding across the blue sky held no answers.

Face it, Raya. You may long for Adonai, but He does not notice you. You are nobody special and your child could do nothing for Israel. The Philistines control us. What can one child do? Even one with the greatest gifts and most strength cannot free us from the grasp of evil pagan worshippers who do all they can to oppress us.

Israel was getting what it deserved from the Philistine oppression, for everyone knew—those who still cared about God's laws—that most of Israel had done evil in His sight. They never learned, though oppressors always came when they fell away from God's ways.

She kicked a stone in the path. Forty years of this oppression seemed like forever, and people were weary of it all—*she* was weary of it all. But she couldn't do anything to stop their enemies any more than she could turn light to darkness. And any child she might bear certainly could do nothing. Israel needed a great leader and a large army, but the nation was too disjointed, like Raya's own thoughts and emotions.

They reached the well, and she shoved her longing thoughts aside. "I'm glad you came," she said, glancing at Talia. "Perhaps when we return, we can help Karmela for a change. If she will let us."

"She will let us this time, I think. At least until she has everything under control." Talia lowered her jar and pulled it up dripping and sweating along the sides. Raya did the same and the two began the trek homeward.

"I will do whatever she needs," Raya said, denying the kick of jealousy and guilty hope that Karmela would refuse their help and leave them to weave in peace. But as they approached the house and heard the commotion of children and Karmela shouting and Adah's voice adding to the clamor, Raya wished she could retract her promise to help and run to the fields to pray.

Sometimes a day did not go the way it should.

Raya slipped away from the house midafternoon to finally fulfill her longed-for time alone. The breeze whipped against the headscarf and she fought its force toward a copse of trees not far from home, yet far enough to drown out the noise of the household and allow her to think. At her approach, the branches swayed as if in greeting. She stepped into a clearing and the wind quieted but for the swish of the leaves. A turn toward the fields gave her a better view, but a moment later, a blinding light blocked her vision. She looked heavenward. Had the sun suddenly broken through her sanctuary and sent a shaft of its light to warm her?

The light moved, and a few moments later, she saw the outline of a man. The urge to scream rose in her throat but as the man grew visible, she knew this was no ordinary person. The glow encasing him was like that of an angel. His bearing and size, larger and taller than two men, sent her to her knees. Raya planted her face to the earth, and an uncontrollable shaking moved through her from head to toe. *Who are you?*

Surely he was not of this world. Was she imagining him? If she opened her tightly shut eyes, would he disappear?

Raya. Had he called her name? She lifted her head, cautious, trembling. And then she was suddenly kneeling, her gaze lifted upward, as if he had tipped her chin without her realizing it.

"Even though you have been unable to have children," the man said, his voice deep yet nearly a whisper in her ear, "you will soon become pregnant and give birth to a son. So be careful; you must not drink wine or any other alcoholic drink nor eat any forbidden food. You will become pregnant and give birth to a son, and his hair must never be cut. For he will be dedicated to God as a Nazirite from birth. He will begin to rescue Israel from the Philistines."

I'm going to have a son? She wanted to ask him aloud, but in a moment he disappeared, the light no longer blinding her. What had she witnessed? She glanced at the sky peeking through the trees. *Adonai?*

Surely the visit was from an angel of the Lord. Who but God could tell the future? Who but God would choose her son to be a Nazirite from birth? No other culture understood the call of a Nazirite. Had she dreamed him? But no. She had just entered the trees when he appeared.

I'm going to have a child. A child. The thought overwhelmed her, and the sudden fear and joy of it rushed through her, bringing the melody of song to her lips. *Praise You, Adonai! Praise be to Your name!*

A tune accompanied her words as she moved from thinking to singing them aloud. She rose slowly and raised her hands to the sky. "How good You are, Adonai!"

She turned then toward the fields where Manoah kept the sheep, lifted her robe above her ankles, and ran toward him with all of her strength. If she were not thinking clearly, Manoah would set her straight and tell her she was tired, overwrought. But if she truly had seen the angel of the Lord, he would believe her words. Her praise would not be without merit.

She ran faster, her breath heaving. She was not sure she wanted to know what he would say, but she knew she would not rest until she told him all that had happened.

CHAPTER TWO

Raya slowed as she came to a rise in the land and stopped to shade her eyes, looking this way and that. Where was he? She knew the various places he took the sheep to pasture, but sometimes grass was thin and he had to walk farther than he normally did.

She drew in a ragged breath, willing her heart to slow its rapid beating. *A baby?* Her spirits lifted again, and she could not stop the joy filling her. Manoah *must* believe her. Adonai would not let her down.

She walked and half ran, then at last saw him in the distance and raced toward him, holding her side for the effort. She came up beside him and placed her hands on her knees, pulling in deep breaths of air.

"Raya! Woman, what are you doing running across the field like that? You could have tripped or turned an ankle or fallen or...worse." Manoah's look held concern, and his dark brows drew down into a slight frown. "Is everything well?"

Raya lifted her head, feeling the flush in her face from her hurry, and smiled into his eyes. She came closer, longing to fall into his arms, but she knew too well that Manoah preferred she saved her affection for the privacy of their home. Never mind that only his brother was somewhere nearby. Still, she held back and simply touched his hand and squeezed.

"I have news!" The joy burst from her again, and a smile lit her face. "A man of God appeared to me! He looked like one of God's angels, terrifying to see. I didn't ask where he was from, and he didn't tell me his name. But he told me, 'You will become pregnant and give birth to a son. You must not drink wine or any other alcoholic drink nor eat any forbidden food. For your son will be dedicated to God as a Nazirite from the moment of his birth until the day of his death.'"

Had he said all of that? Perhaps she did not remember exactly. Had he mentioned the boy's death? Or was he only to be a Nazirite for most of his life? There was no indication the vow would ever be revoked, so to add her words—did she add them?—made sense in a strange, sad way. In that instant, she could almost envision his birth, though his death lay hidden from her mind. *Please, Adonai, do not let me outlive this child.* She could not bear the thought of burying him, even though she had yet to give birth to him. Soon?

"Do you believe me?" She searched Manoah's face for some sign of acceptance, understanding. "Please, Manoah, if you think I have lost my senses, tell me. But I know what I saw and heard from his lips, and I do not think I was dreaming."

He cupped her cheek. "Even if you had been dreaming, obviously you dreamed something from the Lord. I have never known you to think senselessly, Raya. I believe you."

She smiled and released a sigh, relieved. *Thank You, Adonai.*

"But I think we should pray. For to confirm your words, a husband is to either say something or remain silent in acceptance. I would like to know my part in this, and how are we supposed to raise the child exactly as the Lord requires?" He ran a hand over his beard, his expression filled with concern. "I do not want to fail our God."

She touched his arm. "You are a good man, Manoah, my husband. You will not fail our God."

"Nevertheless, kneel with me to pray." He took her hand and set his staff on the ground and together they knelt in the dirt.

"Lord," Manoah prayed, "please let the man of God come back to us again and give us more instructions about this son who is to be born."

He lifted his hands to heaven and together they gazed upward to the place where God lived. Would the angel appear to them right away? Raya's heart pounded at the thought, recalling the terror mingled with the joy of his words. She waited beside her husband as they searched the sky and fields and at last rose to their feet, glancing about them.

"Perhaps He will answer at a later time," Raya said, seeing the slight disappointment fill Manoah's gaze. "Who can understand God's ways or His timing?"

Manoah looked toward the grazing sheep, the soft bleating coming from a few of them, sounds of chewing distant but familiar. This was the life her husband had always known, and she had always dreamed of giving him a son to follow in his footsteps. But a Nazirite? How would such a child also be a shepherd? Or would God give him a different calling? There were so many things she wanted to ask, and yet despite Manoah's prayer, God did not seem to hear. No angel appeared to them then and there.

"Do you still believe me?" Raya clasped her hands in front of her and gazed at him, entreating him with a look. *Please believe me.* She lived with enough strife in her father-in-law's household. She did not wish to live in conflict or differing opinions with the one she loved most.

"I still believe you," he said at last. He stepped forward, and she thought he would pick up his staff. But he pulled her close instead, surprising her. She wrapped her arms about his neck.

"Thank you, husband. I feared you would not." Raya kissed his cheek.

"Because He did not answer me immediately?" Manoah leaned away from her.

She nodded. "I admit the thought crossed my mind."

He placed his hands on either side of her face and kissed her briefly. "Beloved, just because our God does not immediately answer our prayers does not mean that He has not heard. Sometimes He waits to test us. Sometimes He is silent for reasons only He knows. But we prayed in earnest with honest questions. When He is ready, He will respond in His own way. We must be ready for it."

She took his hands and cradled them in hers. "Thank you. You always help me to keep hoping. And to wait, even when I do not want to."

He laughed, lifting their twined hands to his lips and kissed her fingers. "I only tell you what I have learned in this life on the earth. The rest of our people may not trust Him or even believe He is watching us do whatever we think is right, but I still believe His laws and know He is just. His way is right. And we will know His answer when He is ready to tell us." He released her hands and touched her nose with his long finger. "Go home now and do what you must. I will be there soon. And perhaps later..." His look held more than he was willing to say.

She laughed. Perhaps later they would do what they could to fulfill the angel's words. She could read his desire in a glance. "I will be waiting for you." She glimpsed her brother-in-law Elead walking toward them, waving, and she smiled one more time at Manoah. Her gait was light and full of hope the entire walk home.

A week passed, and Raya sat at her loom weaving colorful threads for a new cloak for Manoah. His was nearly threadbare, and though he never complained, she knew when the winds blew he would appreciate a warmer cloak.

The door to their part of the house opened, and Adah stepped into the room, her gaze assessing. "It is coming along nicely. How soon do you expect it to be finished? Manoah could surely use it even now." His mother's look held censure, as if Raya should have begun the project sooner or been done with it by now. Never mind the time it took to sheer the sheep, spin the wool, pick the flowers for the dye, then dye separate batches into different colors, and when at last all was ready, weave the threads into the beautiful garment she intended. Adah knew this.

"You know I have worked diligently, *Imma* Adah. The cloak will be ready in time for cooler weather." She bit her lip against words she wished she could say. *Adonai, forgive me.* She struggled to understand Adah's questions, which felt like meddling, when she was probably just concerned and protective of her son as she had always been. It was a mother's way, she told herself, though without a child of her own, she could not know for sure.

"I'm sure you will, my dear. I just thought I would stop in to see your progress." Adah sank onto one of the cushions, obviously planning a lengthier stay. "You know, when Manoah was a small boy, I had my hands full with three sons, so to keep up with the spinning and weaving and cooking and all that goes into keeping a home nearly wore me out. Baruch's mother, peace be upon her, was more helpful than I realized at the time. I don't think I could have done everything without her, for Baruch had only sisters and no sister-in-law to help run our household." She fingered the basket of yarns, examining the different colors. "You might learn something from this."

Raya met her gaze, feeling the slight sting of rebuke. Did Adah want her to come to her for help weaving and spinning? Or was she asking for something more? She lifted a brow. "What are you saying, Imma Adah? I have no children for you to help me raise, nor am I needed overmuch with the meals with Karmela taking charge of things. I am not sure what you want of me." She liked Adah well enough, but sometimes the woman confused her.

"Only that it would be nice of you to invite me to visit or help you now and then. I don't want to help the others and neglect you, my dear." She looked beyond Raya, as if she wanted to say more but hesitated. At last she stood. "It is simply nice to be wanted, and I want you to know that I want you and hope you feel the same." She stepped closer and patted Raya's shoulder then turned and left the room.

Raya stared at the closed door and allowed the shuttle to ease to a stop. The loom stood silent, accusing her—the same feeling that had washed over her in Adah's presence. Why did she feel thus? Her mother-in-law simply wanted to encourage her. Didn't she?

Restlessness suddenly overtook her, and she pushed herself away from the loom and stood. After grabbing her cloak from a peg on the wall, she wrapped it about her and left through the side door. The afternoon breeze was warm, and the sun kissed her cheeks as if in greeting. She lifted her gaze, watching the wispy clouds race across a blue sky.

She walked swiftly toward the clearing in the trees, then decided against it and walked to a field beyond it. Somehow she could not bring herself to revisit the place where the angel had come, since he had not returned, though it had been a week since Manoah had asked God to send him.

Perhaps she had dreamed the vision. There was no sign that she carried a child, though she had not given her body enough time to know for certain. Still, the lack of confirmation caused an ache deep within her, an unsettled feeling that perhaps she wanted this child so badly she had imagined everything in her desperate need.

She sank onto a grassy spot, knees to her chest, and buried her head against them. *Oh, Adonai, forgive me. If I have imagined what I want to be true and it is not, please forgive Your maidservant. But if You truly did come to visit me, won't You hurry to answer Manoah's prayer? Or if You will not hurry, at least please help me to stop wrestling with the longing and the waiting and the feeling as though I am deceived.*

She paused her prayer, hoping for a sense of peace, when suddenly the light shifted as it had the week before, and a blinding shaft of brilliant white invaded the space near her. She lifted her head and saw him again, a man, yet not a man, clothed in white so bright no one could duplicate it on earth. His eyes pierced hers, and her whole body trembled as it had the first time. Terror and joy mingled in her spirit, and she could not force her limbs to move.

But as she dared to meet his gaze, rather than glance beyond him, she felt immediately safe and her strength returned. *I must get Manoah.* She did not speak, but the man seemed to read her thoughts, for he moved his arm in the direction Manoah worked with the sheep.

She jumped to her feet, nodded to the man, and ran again across the field until she came to Manoah, breathless. "He came!" She gasped and took a drink of water from the skin he handed to her. "The man who appeared to me the other day is here again!"

Manoah did not hesitate, nor even look to see if Elead could watch his sheep, but took her hand and raced the distance to the place where she had left the angel. Manoah heaved a great sigh when they saw he had waited.

Manoah approached, eyes wide and awestruck. "Are you the man who spoke to my wife the other day?"

"Yes," the angel replied, "I am."

Manoah sank to his knees and lifted his hands in entreaty. "When your words come true, what kind of rules should govern the boy's life and work?"

"Be sure your wife follows the instructions I gave her," he said. "She must not eat grapes or raisins, drink wine or any other alcoholic drink, or eat any forbidden food."

Manoah nodded but did not speak for a moment, as if processing the man's words. Raya lifted her gaze to search the man's features, wondering why he had not answered Manoah's specific question but rather directed his response at her. How was her behavior going to help them know how to raise the child or what rules the boy should follow?

Thoughts whirled in her mind when Manoah finally spoke. "Please stay here until we can prepare a young goat for you to eat."

He did not ask the angel to explain things better? She longed to do so herself but knew it was not her place to ask in her husband's stead. She looked between the two, awaiting the angel's response.

"I will stay," the angel of the Lord said, "but I will not eat anything. However, you may prepare a burnt offering as a sacrifice to the Lord."

Manoah nodded, and Raya watched them both, overcome with too many emotions. "Go home and prepare a grain offering," the angel said, looking at her.

She turned and ran home as he directed while Manoah raced back to where he had left the sheep. It took time to pull the grain from the sack, sift out the stones, grind it into fine flour, and mix it with olive oil. She took care to bake the flatbread on the three-pronged griddle, break it into pieces when it had cooled, and pour olive oil over it again.

At last finished, she placed the pieces in a flaxen basket lined with linen and raced back across the field. But as she came in sight of the angel, she saw that Manoah had just returned with a year-old goat. No doubt it had taken him time to choose one without blemish.

She came toward him, ever aware of the angel watching them. Manoah placed the animal between them and inspected it as if he had not already done so. "Perfect, as I thought," he said softly.

He and Raya placed their hands on the head of the animal, but before Manoah pulled the knife from his belt, he looked again at the angel. "What is your name? For when all this comes true, we want to honor you."

Raya's heart beat faster at the question. The man—angel— had said nothing of his name the first time, nor when he arrived this time. Why would Manoah ask it of him? To honor him was good, but would the man answer?

"Why do you ask my name?" The angel's voice deepened, like whispered thunder. "It is too wonderful for you to understand."

Manoah did not respond, though Raya saw his face flush, and she wondered if he wished he had not asked the question. He left the goat with Raya then found a large rock and dragged it closer. Raya walked the goat toward him, the grain offering in her other hand, and as she placed the offering on the rock, Manoah slit the goat's throat, drained its blood, and placed it on the rock as well.

Flames immediately shot upward from the rock altar, reaching to the sky, and the angel of the Lord ascended into the sky amid the flames.

Raya cried out, and together they fell to their knees, faces pressed into the earth. "It was surely the angel of the Lord," Manoah said. "We will certainly die, for we have seen God!"

Raya, still trembling, slowly lifted her head and glanced about her. The fire had burned the entire sacrifice and left only black ashes in its wake. There was no sign of the angel again, but this time, she had no doubt that she had not imagined him. Manoah had spoken to him, and to see him rise into the heavens… She could not put the experience into words even in the silence of her heart.

She looked at her husband and took his hand, her mind still whirling with all she had seen but knowing she must comfort and assure him. "If the Lord were going to kill us, He wouldn't have accepted our burnt offering and grain offering. He wouldn't have appeared to us and told us this wonderful thing and done these miracles."

Manoah squeezed her hand, and she could feel the shaking that had swept through him. "Of course you are right." He looked slowly around him, lingered long in gazing at the altar, then lifted his face toward the heavens. "For reasons I do not understand, God has chosen us, Beloved." He looked at her and touched her cheek. "A child. So simple yet so impossible for us. And yet God has heard our prayers and given us this promise. What kind of man will our son be?"

Raya drew close and rested her head on his shoulder. "I do not know, my husband. But I believe he will be used of God for some great purpose. Why else would God visit us so? Though first he will be a small babe in need of our guidance." She leaned away to look into his dark, penetrating eyes. "I am sure you will be a great teacher for him."

"May he always obey the laws of our God." Manoah kissed the top of her head then pulled her to her feet.

"And the laws of the Nazirite," Raya added. To raise such a child would be a daunting task. But she chose not to think about that now. Now only one thought occupied her mind. She was no longer to be known as a barren woman. She would bear a child—a son!

She could think of no greater blessing.

CHAPTER THREE

One Year Later

Raya traced her finger over the soft downy skin of her son as he nursed at her breast. Three months old and already he had a thick head of dark hair, nearly black in color as his father's used to be. Yet even Adah had exclaimed over how fast the boy's hair had grown since the day of his birth, when he had barely a hair to cover his round head.

How long would it grow over a lifetime if she could already lift it from his forehead to his ear? Samson. She had chosen the name at his circumcision, in memory of the angel who had announced his birth and whose appearance shone brighter than the sun. Would Samson's life shine like the sun as his name implied?

He pulled away and she raised him to her shoulder and patted his back. How fast he had grown in only three months! *Please, Adonai, do not let him grow up too quickly. Allow me the joy of relishing his childhood before manhood overtakes him.*

It was a foolish prayer, a selfish prayer really. But after waiting so long to be able to bear a child, she suddenly could not consider the thought of him ever leaving her. Was that so wrong?

A check in her spirit told her it was. She needed to prepare herself for a future when he would one day leave her. But as she held him away from her to look into his eyes and shifted sides, his slight contented smile melted her heart once more. Not today. She still had him today and she would think about tomorrow when it came time to teach him the ways of Adonai and the vow that had been entrusted to him.

A knock on her door pulled her gaze from marveling at her son. "Come in," she called softly, so as not to upset him.

Talia poked her head around the door. "Are you welcoming company?"

"If it is just you." She smiled as her sister-in-law opened and softly closed the door behind her. "I'm afraid too many people at once will cause him to cry."

Talia sank onto a cushion across from Raya. "Is he sleeping better for you yet? I have not heard his cries in the night."

"I try to snatch him up before he cries too loudly. I wake at the first sound he makes." Raya closed her eyes for a brief moment. "I must admit his lack of sleep wears me out. Perhaps that is why God usually gives babies to younger women." She chuckled.

"You are not so old. Why, you could have more children after Samson is weaned. Look at Sarah. You are hardly close to ninety!" Talia's musical laugh caused Raya to join in. Samson pulled his mouth from nursing at the sound. His lower lip puckered, and Raya braced herself for a loud wail.

"We've done it now," she said, as Samson made full use of his lungs. She stood and walked about the small room, patting his back, saying soothing words in his ear.

"Do you want me to take him?" Talia also stood and held her arms out to Raya. "It is obvious that you could use some sleep. He is fed now, so let me take him out of your rooms so you can rest."

Raya held him closer, suddenly protective, but she *was* tired. Unutterably so. At last she handed Samson to his aunt along with a blanket and extra linens. "He will need changing."

Talia smiled. "I've had practice. This will be good to remind me why *I'm* too old to have another!"

Raya touched her son's soft hair and kissed his cheek, finally allowing Talia to take him from the room. His cries continued as she lay on her mat and tried to ignore them, telling herself that this was a kind offer and she must trust other people with her son. She could not be at his side for the rest of his life. She could not always keep him safe. But he was still so small. He needed her. That thought filled her as she attempted sleep, certain it would not come, surprised when she awoke an hour later to find Samson asleep beside her and Talia spinning in her small sitting area nearby.

Raya rose, rubbing the sleep from her eyes, and joined Talia after taking a long look at her sweet son.

"He was asleep within a few moments after I left you. I suspect watching Karmela chop vegetables bored him to sleep." Talia let the spindle wind down to switch threads.

"I must thank Karmela for the extra time she has taken to see that I eat well. She has been so helpful in keeping grapes and raisins from our diet." Raya had thanked her, but she should do so again when she joined the family for the evening meal. She had a new appreciation for her formerly frustrating sister-in-law, though she still wondered how the woman could care so little about anything except the daily chores of life.

"She has been good about that," Talia said, threading a new color onto the spindle. "I wonder how you are going to keep Samson from tasting those forbidden foods when he grows old enough to want them."

Raya had often wondered that very thing all throughout her pregnancy. "I am glad we live in a household that obeys the dietary laws of God. But you are right. Most families are allowed to eat grapes, and raisin cakes are a popular treat. Even if he avoids wine, it will be hardest to keep him from the rest."

"If he ever travels into Philistine territory, he will have to decide for himself whether to avoid our forbidden foods. They eat so many animals that don't chew the cud that we won't even touch." Talia began spinning again, and Raya's arms felt suddenly as though she needed to do something useful. She moved to the neglected loom and continued to weave a small garment for Samson, as she had long since finished Manoah's new cloak.

"Why do you suggest he will go to the Philistines?" Talia had never said such a thing before this moment, and Raya could not bear the thought of her son mingling with the foreigners who had oppressed their nation for forty years. And yet, might Samson's miraculous birth and separating vow have something to do with their downfall? Hadn't the angel said he would begin to rescue Israel from the Philistines? But she had not told Talia that.

Talia shrugged. "I don't know. I just think Samson was born for a reason. And Manoah indicated to Elead that the angel you saw said he would rescue us from the Philistine domination."

So Manoah had told his brother, while she had kept the words close to her heart. She sighed, understanding now. "The angel only said that the boy would begin to rescue Israel from the Philistines. I don't believe he meant that Samson will necessarily complete that rescue in his lifetime."

"But if he can rally the men to fight like Joshua of old, perhaps he will. He could turn out to be one of Israel's greatest leaders, Raya. Doesn't that thought thrill you?" Talia's perpetual joyful expression lifted Raya's dragging spirit. When *she* thought of her son leaving her or going to the Philistine encampments or cities for any reason, a shudder worked through her as though she could already feel the fear of what could happen to him. It was worry, plain and simple, and she could not fear now what was such a long way off.

"I..." She paused, concentrated on the shuttle a moment, then looked at Talia. "I admit the thought of him leading any army, or however God plans to use him to rescue us, does not thrill me. It scares me." She let her hands fall from the shuttle. "Oh, Talia, how do you stay so happy about these things? I've waited so long for a child and now to have God finally hear and answer is both wonderful and terrifying. Why us? Why must our son be a Nazirite and future leader to fulfill a purpose that will put him in the way of much possible harm? What if he is killed before he can exact any sort of revenge or deliverance?"

Talia continued her spinning as though it took no thought, but her gaze never left Raya's face. "Dear Raya. I know Karmela does not fear our God as we would like, but you do! You have always prayed to Him and cared to keep His laws and pondered His ways. And now that He has given you your heart's desire, you fear? Do you not think that the God who made your son can also keep him safe? Keep him in His care until he completes the work he was born to do? And that you will live to see it and be glad?"

Raya studied her hands, unable to hold Talia's gaze. She used to trust so easily. She was the one assuring Manoah when he feared or doubted. But now that it concerned her son, the fruit of her body, she had an overwhelming need to protect him against everything. Against evil. Against those who might do him harm. And most of all against himself, for she did not know if he would be strong enough in character to keep these vows he did not ask to be given.

"You are right." She looked up, feeling as though she had allowed the silence to linger too long. "But I do not share your hope that I will live to see him do great things. We cannot know how long we have on this earth. It may be that I will rest with my ancestors long before Samson grows old enough to know right from wrong."

"Don't say such things, Raya. You are not yourself." Talia let the spindle come to a stop and came to sit beside Raya. She placed a hand on Raya's arm. "Dear one, you are still recovering from birth. I know it has been three months, but sometimes it takes a woman longer to feel normal again, especially since Samson's sleep is still not long enough for you to take your rest as you should. So put these foolish thoughts from your mind. Of course you will live to raise your son and teach him right from wrong. Why else would God have given him to you if not for you and Manoah to raise?" She patted Raya's arm and then pulled her into a warm embrace. "You must not fret, my sister. You will see in a few more months that what you are feeling is normal and all of us who have borne children have felt the same. You will soon return to the trust you once had." She held Raya at arm's length. "Promise me?"

Raya nodded. "I promise." She smiled. "Thank you. You are right. I have been so tired and overwrought and every worry I have ever had seems to be attacking me like a swarm of bees lately."

"It is all part of having a child." Talia cupped Raya's cheek. "You will be fine. You will see."

"I hope so. And I hope it is soon." At that moment, Samson stirred in the small basket Manoah had made for him. "Though it looks like I am needed again."

"Wait a moment and see if he is simply moving in his sleep," she whispered.

They waited in silence, and the quiet descended again. Raya blew out a breath. "Peace for a little longer," she said softly.

"Yes. And I think you should take a walk outside right now before he must nurse again. I will stay with him." She stood and pulled Raya to her feet. "Go on. It will do you good."

Raya glanced back at her son, then donned her sandals, grabbed her cloak, and mouthed a silent thank-you to Talia.

She slipped into the afternoon warmth, allowed the sun to drench her upturned face, and closed her eyes against its glare. Talia was right. She needed this short time away and she needed to stop worrying. Perhaps what she needed most was time to walk and talk with Adonai as she used to do before Samson's birth. She set off toward her clearing to do just that.

Five Years Later

"Why do my cousins get to go to the grape treading while I must stay here with you?" Samson crossed his small arms and looked into Raya's eyes, hurt and anger causing a deepening frown.

Raya drew a breath and gently took her five-year-old's hand and tugged him toward a bench in the courtyard where she had been grinding grain to help while Karmela and the others had gone off to the grape harvest. She coaxed him to sit, though by the stubborn set of his chin she knew he sat under protest. She knelt at his side and met him at eye level.

"We've talked about this before, my love. You and Imma cannot eat grapes or drink wine or eat anything unclean. You cannot touch a dead body or cut your hair, for you were called by God to be a Nazirite since before you were born. An angel of the Lord has given you this blessing and calling. We must not go to the harvest, lest we are tempted to disobey the Lord." She searched his face. "I know it is not easy for you to watch your cousins run off and do things you cannot, but they are not blessed of the Lord as you are. Your life will be different and you will do great things with God's power. You just have to wait until you are a little older. Do you understand, Samson?"

He stared at her, the stubborn look still visible in his dark eyes. How beautiful this child was, his lashes long, his hair already below his shoulders. She had taken to braiding it lest it get caught in a tree limb and be yanked out. She took great pains to make sure he kept Adonai's laws, but she could not make his heart want to obey them.

The thought troubled her too often, despite his young age. "Do you understand?" she asked again.

He slowly nodded, his shoulders slumping in apparent defeat. "It is hard, Imma. I *want* to eat the raisin cakes Aunt Karmela sometimes makes, and my cousins tease me with clusters of grapes and hold them in front of me. I want to yank the grapes away and push my cousins down." His gaze shifted to his feet then, as if the admission embarrassed him. "I know I shouldn't because you would be angry, so I don't."

A deep sense of sorrow filled her with his words. "Oh Samson." She sat beside him and pulled him onto her lap. "I would not be angry, my son. Only sorry that you felt so hurt by your cousins that you would want to hurt them back. They should not treat you that way."

His head lifted and his eyes widened. "So it's all right if I push them down?"

She laughed softly and shook her head. "No, no. That's not what I meant. It's not right to seek to hurt other people, especially your family. Someday it might be all right to hurt the Philistines because God called you to rescue our people from them because they are hurting us. But you mustn't hurt our people, even if they are mean to you. They just don't understand that you are different because you are blessed by God."

His lower lip puckered even as he fisted both small hands. "It doesn't feel like I'm blessed, Imma." He laid his head on her shoulder as he did before he was weaned, something she missed of late.

"I know, Beloved. Sometimes when God calls us, people do not understand us. Perhaps what is a blessing to us makes them jealous because they don't have the same blessing." How to make a child understand? Even she didn't understand the awesome, holy blessing of their God.

"I still want to eat grapes and raisins," he said, pouting now. "And I'm still not glad to miss the grape treading." He slid from her lap and looked at her, obvious confusion in his eyes. "I don't think I want God's blessing. Can I give it back?"

She forced herself not to laugh at his innocent request. How hard it must be for him to avoid things everyone else ate without thought. She didn't eat them now that he was weaned simply to help him, to show him that not *everyone* was different from him. But they were. And so was she, despite her efforts.

She stood and took his hand, leading him away from the house. "Why don't we go to the fields to visit Abba? You love the sheep, and I am sure he could use your help."

He brightened at that, and she released a relieved sigh. But as they neared the fields where Manoah watched the sheep and goats, he looked up at her again. "I still want to give it back," he said. Then he let go of her hand and ran toward his father, leaving her feeling bereft of his presence and worried. So very worried.

CHAPTER FOUR

Raya entered the cooking area in the central courtyard of her father-in-law's sprawling household, where Karmela, Talia, and Adah were already at work. Raya could have joined them sooner, but she'd lingered, watching Manoah and Samson call the sheep and a handful of goats to follow them. Samson had grown quickly in the past few years, and she could no longer keep him with her. He was taller than most boys of twelve and belonged with his father. Manoah would teach him the skill of shepherding, something he should learn whether he ever followed in his father's path or not.

"Welcome, Raya," Talia said, her ever-present smile filling her wide face. The woman wasn't beautiful as some saw beauty, but Raya had never known anyone with a more pleasing and cheerful attitude.

"It's a wonder you've come at all," Karmela said, the hint of her old sarcasm in her voice. Though Ariel, Manoah's younger brother, had married this woman of charm, her beauty was on the surface. If only God could help her hold that sometimes caustic tongue!

"I was detained," Raya said, not willing to divulge why. Everyone except Talia already thought she doted too much on Samson.

"Humph." Karmela set to mixing the flour she had already ground with olive oil and rolled it out, stamping her handprint in the center to spread it into flatbread.

"It is good you have come, dear," Adah said, passing a bowl of lentils to her. "You can sift for stones."

Raya took the clay bowl from her and began the laborious task of sifting. They wouldn't begin to cook the lentils for hours, but it took time to pick and cut the vegetables from the garden and prepare the stew for such a large household. With Samson's appetite, Raya had been forced to help more if only out of guilt. He'd grown so fast she could not decide whether to weave larger garments or cook more food.

"Elead tells me that Samson is becoming quite the shepherd. Though I wonder how often our husbands have to keep the boys from running off to play rather than watch the sheep." Talia looked over her shoulder as she spoke, then turned back to the water trough, where she rinsed the dirt from the leeks, garlic, dill, and onions.

"Samson is turning into a fine boy," Adah said, her praise surprising Raya. His grandmother so rarely complimented him or praised them for how they were raising him. "I must admit, I don't understand why he must remain a Nazirite, but if that is what my son wants, that's what he will be." She looked at Karmela. "It would help if your sons did not taunt the boy with raisin cakes though, my daughter. But more importantly, we should not be making them in the first place. Why did you start to make them again when you did not during Raya's pregnancy?"

Raya looked from Adah to Karmela, whose cheeks had reddened. The taunting *had* continued, despite Raya's attempts to ask Karmela to make them stop. And Karmela seemed to enjoy making the special treat on a weekly basis. Manoah simply shrugged and said the boy needed to learn to stand up under such pressure because as he aged it would only get worse. Raya still felt the sting of his reproof when she'd repeatedly asked him to intervene, and one day he'd had enough of her asking.

But to have Adah join her side? *Adonai? Is this Your doing?*

"I've asked them to stop," Karmela said, her tone defensive. "You know how boys are. They don't listen to their mother."

"Then I will speak to Ariel," Adah said, her words carrying a sharp edge. "If their mother cannot control them, their father must. But you, my daughter, must stop making these treats so often. You are hurting Samson." She tossed another handful of grain onto the grinding wheel, and soon the noise of the grinding drowned out their attempts to talk.

Raya focused on the lentils, her thoughts churning. Karmela's anger seeped from her, filling the court with tension, but Adah seemed oblivious, while Talia kept her back turned, paying much more attention to the vegetables than she normally did.

The desire to escape the courtyard and walk in the fields rose within Raya, strong as a mighty wind. But she fought the need. One did not run from difficult people. They stayed and talked things out. But what happened when the other person was not willing to listen? She had tried time after time to reason with Karmela. But as the years had passed Karmela had just grown more defensive. After Adah's rebuke would she change? And what could Raya possibly do about it?

She searched her heart, silently asking God for wisdom. At last, the grinding stone stopped, and Raya spoke before Adah could begin again. "Karmela, may I say something to you?"

Karmela scowled, but she held her gaze. Raya felt Talia's and Adah's gazes also focused on her. "I know it is hard for you to prepare different food for my Samson when it would be so much easier if he could eat the raisin cakes and grapes and other treats we are so used to enjoying as a family. But you have tried, and I wanted to thank you for that. I will do more to find treats that please him—perhaps pistachios and honey, which he seems to favor."

Karmela offered a slight nod. "I do what I can. You have not made it easy with this vow of yours."

"I know that." She had long ago stopped trying to explain to her family that the vow came from the angel of the Lord, for none but Manoah and perhaps Talia believed her. "But since the vow is his and as far as we know now, there is no end to it, we need to support him as best we can. It would mean a lot to Manoah and me if all of us could stand with Samson as he tries to obey the Nazirite laws. It is imperative that he not break them." She lifted her hands in entreaty, searching each woman's face.

"You know you have our support," Talia said, her expression earnest, even if she didn't fully understand.

"You have ours as well," Adah added. "We will stand by our grandson as we have with all of our grandchildren."

Karmela looked beyond her, as though she was not sure she could be part of this family pact of support. Raya prayed, her heart longing to share this faith with her sister-in-law. Somehow, Karmela simply could not understand that one could love God and have a relationship with Him, not just follow His laws. To her, faith was simply obeying the Law of Moses. But Raya knew it was so much more.

At last Karmela looked at Raya. "I have a pistachio treat that I save for feast days, but I think we can change it enough to make it easier to have more often."

Raya smiled. "Thank you, Karmela."

The woman simply nodded then returned to making a pile of flatbread to toss onto the griddle. It wasn't a giant change of attitude or a moment of her sister-in-law finally understanding their God the way Raya longed for her to do, but it was a start. If they could be civil to each other, perhaps they could become friendlier. And with such a challenging son like Samson, who sometimes still chafed at his unrequested vow, Raya welcomed all the friends she could get.

Samson walked ahead of his cousins and father, expecting the few sheep his father had put into his care to follow. The wind picked up, whipping his coat about him, and he felt the glory of his own strength as he gripped the staff and called the sheep by name.

"Come on," he yelled above the wind. Dust blew from areas where the sheep had munched the grass to the roots. In the distance behind him, voices called to him. He turned.

"Samson, wait for us. We need to get the animals to a shelter to wait out this storm." His father waved as he shouted, and his uncle and cousins were hurrying to herd the sheep and goats to catch up to Samson.

Samson turned back to scan the hills up ahead. A number of caves stood out, hopefully empty of bodies or bandits or wild animals asleep at the back. He called his sheep and motioned to his family to follow. Home was some distance away, as they'd had to travel farther to find pasture during the past few days. Now the east winds, infrequent though they were, had kicked up, trapping them from getting back to their sheep pens and brick houses.

Samson tucked his head forward and stopped, allowing his sheep to catch up to his long strides, then urged them forward. Moments later his father, uncle, and cousins joined him, and they fought the wind to reach the caves, speaking only to the sheep and goats to calm them.

When at last they reached the caves, Samson stepped inside each one and looked them over. Some were small and would not hold many of their animals. "We will have to divide up," he said, turning to his father.

"Unless we move the stone on that one. It can't be a burial cave, as it is not fully blocked. It may be large enough for all of us." Manoah looked back at the others, who nodded their agreement.

Samson strode toward the blocked cave and peered inside. Darkness told him the cave went back farther than the others. Wild animals could be sleeping in the interior. He had no light that would not have blown out, but suddenly he had no fear, only a heightened determination. He would please his father by doing this, so he bent down, lifted the heavy boulder and set it to the side of the cave. Then he stepped inside, let his eyes adjust to the dark, and walked toward the back.

The walls and floor were dry, a good sign. He saw no bats hanging from the ceiling or animal dung as far as the light coming from the cave opening would allow him to see. He continued farther in, barely hearing his father call his name and warn him to be careful.

Of course he would be careful. Hadn't his mother taught him thus over and over again all of his life? True, he was just barely a man by Israelite standards, but he could tell by his body's changes that he was taller and stronger, and he was not afraid. Fear was for the weak, and Samson had begun to realize that he was not weak. God, who had given him this vow from birth, must have included strength as one of the blessings for his obedience.

Perhaps the vow wasn't such a terrible thing, as he'd felt in his restricted childhood. If he could lift a boulder as though it were as light as sheep's wool newly shorn, what more could he do?

He continued deeper into the cave, eyes darting to the right and left, adjusting more fully now to the dark, when up ahead he saw a small shaft of light coming from above, illuminating the area. So this cave's ceiling was not as thick as others might be. He stood on tiptoe to reach the small hole and pushed against it. Dirt crumbled to the ground, but the ceiling did not cave in. He held back on pushing against it with his full strength, but if they did not venture to this area, they should be safe until the winds died down.

He looked beyond the open area where he stood and walked a little farther until he came to the cave's end. Nothing. No one inhabited the area and there were no side tunnels leading to hidden places where an animal might make its den.

He turned about and came to his family and the sheep again, all still huddling close. "It appears sound and empty," he said smiling. "There is a small hole in the ceiling at the back, but when I gave it a slight push, only a little dirt fell. If we stay to the front of the cave, we will find enough shelter." He motioned them forward, and they came without question.

When the last of the sheep and goats were inside the cave, his father and uncle began to count the animals. Samson joined them, gently guiding each counted one to move away from the others. His cousins stood watch, keeping the sheep and goats separate from the hundreds still to be counted.

The counting took time, but when they finished, Samson's father looked up. "One of the lambs is missing," he said, drawing a hand down his graying beard. "How could one be missing?"

"It is windy, Abba. Perhaps the wind blew it off course and it followed a different path or fell into a hole in the ground." Samson, who had removed his cloak during the counting, donned it again and wrapped it tightly about himself. He grabbed his staff from leaning against the cave wall. "I will look for it."

"We are fortunate only one is missing," Uncle Elead said.

"Do we really need to look for only one lamb?" his cousin Chaim asked.

"In this wind, Son, it's too dangerous for you. I will go." Samson's father grabbed his staff as well.

Samson placed a hand on his father's shoulder. "I am strong, Abba. I can stand against the wind." He bent closer to his father's ear to avoid ridicule from his cousins. "God is with me, Abba. He will lead me to the lamb."

His father looked at him, eyes widening. It was the first time Samson had mentioned God in that way to his father or mother. But even as he said His name, Samson felt a sense of rightness about his role in this. He *was* called by God to do great things. He knew it deep within himself as he'd never known it before this moment. What more might he do with God's help besides find safe shelter or rescue a lost sheep?

"You are sure?" his father asked, his expression anxious. "If you do not return to me, your mother will never forgive me."

"I am sure." He smiled. "You can tell Imma all about it when I return and we all go home in safety." He turned then and set off, but the wind forced his eyes closed, and he could not take many steps away from the cave. He could not turn around and go back inside now. Not after his bold talk!

He pushed forward, squinting one eye open. He pulled the turban from his head and wrapped it about his face, wrestling with the fabric whipping in the wind. At last, he tied it securely over his mouth and nose and held a hand close to his eyes. He searched the landscape, retracing their steps. It would do no good to call to the lamb, for the khamsin, that roaring, dry wind, would steal his words. And any bleating would never be heard above it.

He pushed forward anyway until he was a good distance from the safety of the cave. The terrain was hilly with small ravines and crevices where a small lamb might have gotten caught. Or brambles along the edges of the hills could catch the wool of a wandering sheep. *Where are you?*

He had to find it. He could not return empty-handed. *Adonai, where is it?*

He glanced at the darkening sky but quickly regretted his choice and ducked his head again into the wind. Yet in that moment, he'd seen something in the distance. Hadn't he?

He dared not look up again lest more grit hit his eyes. Instead, he walked in the direction of what he thought he might have seen, keeping his head down until he drew closer. Then he risked another glance upward, carefully shading both sides of his face. And there, in a line of brambles a lengthy distance from where they had pastured the sheep, he saw the young lamb, bleating pitifully, its wool covered in sand until it was nearly brown instead of white.

Samson stepped close to the brambles, wrapped his cloak around his hands, and tore the thorny bushes away from the lamb's wool, at last freeing it. The animal attempted to scamper away, but the wind would not let it move far. Samson scooped it into his arms, tucked it inside his cloak, and turned back toward the cave where the rest of them waited.

His heart swelled with a sense of gratitude and a bit of pride at his accomplishment. He had done what no one else could have done. Not in this weather or against these elements. The animal bleated plaintively against his chest, and he knew she would need tending with olive oil once she was in the cave. Using his staff for balance, he pushed faster against the wind, cheered by his success. Once he reached the cave, he heard the exclamations of praise and saw the pride in his father's eyes. This was a good day.

CHAPTER FIVE

Raya met Manoah as he returned from speaking to the elders of their town of Zorah. Eight years had come and gone since the days when Samson followed her husband to pasture the sheep, and changes had come to their tribe that troubled every man.

Manoah came into their room, and she took his cloak and hung it on a peg.

"Is Samson with you?" She never knew for sure where he spent his days, though he usually stayed with Manoah when he wasn't out exploring the world outside of their town.

"He is coming," Manoah said. He sank onto a large cushion and removed his turban. "The elders are worried. The Philistines are growing more aggressive, plundering our crops at harvest and stealing our sheep even from the pens. Soon we will be dependent on them for the very food we eat if something is not done to stop them."

Raya nodded. "Samson was born to begin to stop them," she reminded him. "But I'm not sure he knows it yet."

Manoah ran a hand through his graying hair. "He is beginning to know something. Men are coming to him for answers when he sits with me at the gate. We are finding it necessary to spend more time there while Elead and his sons tend the sheep. I think because of Samson's Nazirite appearance and height of stature and great strength, men look to him to lead them, though he is just now the age of a fighting man."

"Do you think Samson will call Israel to war against the Philistines?" She sat beside him but did not pick up her spindle as usual. Karmela would soon call all of them to the evening meal. "I wish your parents had lived to see this." Adah and Baruch had passed into Sheol before Samson reached his twentieth birthday.

"I don't think they would have seen anything, Raya. I do not know if Samson will lead an army to battle. He does not seem to think it will happen and is too content to simply talk about the problems. I've yet to see the Lord stir him to act against our enemies." Manoah rubbed both hands down his face.

"Can we not talk him into doing more? Surely he will listen to us." Raya chafed at the oppression, especially when she knew her son was born for this—to help them all.

"What will we tell him, Raya? He is young. He must be led of God on his own. We cannot make him do anything more than we already have. He has wrestled with being a Nazirite from birth, sometimes loving the calling, sometimes hating it. We cannot ask more of him until God Himself does the leading." He pushed himself up. "I'm hungry. Is it not time for us to eat?"

Raya stood and joined him. "I will go and help Karmela. Find Samson, and by then the food will be ready."

Manoah nodded and followed her out of their room. Samson burst into the house earlier than they expected in his usual boisterous way, laughing with his cousins, who still smelled of sheep. Raya shook her head but hid a secret smile. She loved these moments when they still seemed like boys instead of men. How she wished the time had not gone so quickly and she could keep her son from whatever fate awaited him at God's command. Or at his choice, whichever came to pass.

Grape harvest came again, and Raya intended to remain at home with Samson, as was her custom, lest he be tempted to break his vow. She listened to the laughter and commotion of the household as they prepared to leave to gather the grapes. Wooden baskets would overflow with grapes for the young men to tread in a large limestone vat until the juice ran channeled below, where it could ferment over the next three to five days.

Raya's heart felt its usual kick of nostalgia. She longed to witness the joyous singing and laughter that accompanied such times. Instead, she had remained away for all of Samson's twenty years of life, and he had never experienced this harvest. A sense of gratitude filled her that he could not hear the actual festive moments, as the winepress was a lengthy distance from their house. Perhaps she would take him to the place where she had first met the angel of the Lord and tell him again of the chosen promise of his birth. Yes, that was what she would do. He needed such reminders, as each day she felt him slipping further from her grasp.

She moved from the room she shared with Manoah and walked through the house in search of her son. She would find him raiding the cheeses in the cooking area, no doubt, but when she reached the stores of food, she found no sign of him.

"Samson?" She moved to the general gathering area where the men often sat and discussed their day, but again, found no evidence that Samson was near.

Her heart picked up its pace and kept time with her hurried feet as she moved through every room of the house. Cautiously, she even peeked into the private rooms of her sisters-in-law and their children, hoping, praying that Samson had coaxed a cousin to stay behind with him.

"Samson!" She called his name louder this time as she moved outside to the courtyard and beyond to the fields surrounding the house. But he did not respond to her call.

Fear crawled up her spine, and her sides ached as she ran toward the winepress. The family had gone ahead earlier that morning, and Samson had been with her then. Had he left her without telling her where he was going?

If only Manoah had remained behind with the sheep as he used to do. Why did her husband think it fine that he attend the festival this time while his adult son was forced to avoid it? Didn't he think Samson might follow?

Did he follow?

She ran faster, stopping now and then to catch her breath, slowing as the grapevines came into view and the sounds of singing and the music of tambourines and lyres filled the air. She approached the crowd of her kinsmen and neighbors and saw the young men, loins girded, stomping the grapes as they held onto each other to keep from slipping.

Frantic, she searched the faces of the men in the vat, knees weak with relief when she did not see Samson among them. She drew in a breath then moved slowly through the crowd, looking for her son. His height and long braided hair stood out as she came around the right side of the large vat. He stood near some of the older men, those whose days of stomping the grapes were long past.

"Samson," she said as she came alongside and touched his arm. "Why did you come without telling me?" She shouldn't accuse him in front of the others, but her heart ached with the need to know, and her worry, her intense need to protect him won out over waiting.

"Imma." Samson looked down at her, his brows knit in a frown. "Why do you chase me down? It is not wrong for me to be here. I have not touched a grape, nor joined the young men in the vat." His expression held hurt that she did not trust him, causing her to feel guilt then sadness that he did not see that he could not risk such temptation.

She tugged his arm, beckoning him to follow her, but he held his ground.

"Please, Son, come over here and speak to me where the noise is less and the crowd is thin." Heat crept into her cheeks that her family and neighbors were watching her and hearing their every word.

He looked at her for too long but at last acquiesced and followed her a short distance away.

"Imma, you cannot control me like you did when I was a small child. You cannot keep me at home when I am a man grown. You embarrass me in front of the men who come to me at the city gate when I sit with Abba and judge cases. If I do not come to the festivals, they will no longer respect me." He stroked his long beard and she noticed that he had begun to braid that as well, for it grew unruly to manage.

"I am sorry, my son. I just do not want you to be tempted to break your vow. If you even touch a grape, you may be tempted to taste it. Or sip the wine when it has finished fermenting. I would keep you from the desires that plague us all." She lifted her arms in supplication and touched his cheek, but he turned away.

"I am not a child, Imma. You may not trust me, but you must trust God who has called me. Was it not He who set me among the elders at so young an age? Was it not He who set me apart from birth? If God is with me, He will keep me from such temptation that causes you such fear." His gaze softened when he looked at her and likely saw the hurt in her eyes.

He was right, of course. In the seasons that had changed and made him a man, God had taken him from shepherding the sheep to answering hard questions of the men who came inside their city walls for judgment or help. Though he sat with Manoah, who more often than not left the flocks in the care of their nephews, Raya knew that God seemed to have called Samson to be their next judge. It had been so long since they'd had a judge in Israel that she still struggled with believing this was how Samson would begin to deliver them from the

Philistines. How did sitting and listening to the complaints of his neighbors help them? Any of the elders could do such a thing, as had been their tradition in Israel for as long as there had been cities.

She searched his earnest face, longing to know what thoughts went on behind those fathomless eyes. "I am sorry, Son. I know that I cannot keep you from breaking your vow. And I also know you have the best of intentions to keep it or you would not have left the sheep to begin to lead our people. But I am still your mother, and mothers worry about their children. I would keep you from yourself, for I know that like all men, you are proud and strong and think you will never fall. I want to help you keep that from happening."

"But it's not your place to keep me anymore, Imma." Samson touched her shoulder. "You must stop chasing after me or worrying over my every decision. I want to be here, not to break my vow but to enjoy my family and friends. To celebrate what they are allowed to do and have but I am not."

"Wouldn't you feel better not knowing what you cannot have?" She was pleading now and she knew it, for she longed to make him see reason and the sense behind her words.

But he was shaking his head, and she knew she had lost him, or at least her control of him. And she was not going to get it back.

"I am thinking of moving between Zorah and Eshtaol. One of the men in town has a place in Mahaneh-dan, which he offered to me. I will work the small plot of land and judge the people there, and he will let me stay as long as I like."

He glanced beyond her, as if he knew the news would upset her, especially now. Had he planned this all along? Or was this something he had just heard as he stood with those older men?

"Why did you not tell me this sooner? Does your father know?" If Manoah knew, why did he keep this from her? Her pulse throbbed in her neck and she curled her hands until her nails dug into her palms, fighting the urge to weep.

"You are the first to know," he said gently. "Imma, I only decided a few days ago. I was going to tell you and Abba this evening, but since you are here..."

"And because I've upset you, you would break my heart with such news at a time like this?" Anger surged to the surface—at him—at the man who had made such an offer. "Young men do not leave their father's houses. They bring their brides to live with their families." Why was he doing everything against their traditions? Because he could not follow other things he wanted to follow? To break his vows?

"Not all men, Imma. And I won't be far. If I stay in that crowded house, how can I judge Israel? If I bring a bride to live there, where will we add another room? My cousins are already doing that very thing and there is not going to be enough land for crops if the house keeps growing." He took her hand, his tone softening. "Please understand, Imma. Yes. I am angry that you chase me down like I'm still a child, but no, I am not leaving you because I want to be away from you. I would take you and my father with me if you would come. I just didn't think it would be my place to ask it."

Raya swayed a bit with the sudden revelation of his heart. He held her steady. "You would ask us to live with you?"

"Would it be such an inconvenience?" He smiled, and she could not resist his charm.

"The house is not your own. Why should we leave our home to live in a stranger's place, a place you will not likely stay?" Her mind swirled with too many questioning thoughts.

"Eventually, perhaps I can buy the place. But do not decide now. I must speak to Abba first. We can talk about this more later. For now, might I go back and watch the grape treading? You can trust me, I promise." He cupped her cheek, and she slowly nodded. She could never deny him except where his vow was concerned.

"If you promise." The fear of him failing God surfaced anew, but she pushed it back.

"You can trust me," he said, turning back toward the crowd. "I will be home for dinner."

"I'm staying here," she said, unwilling to let go so finally. "But I will not stand next to you. You may go back to your friends or whoever they are. I will be near."

His chest lifted in a sigh, as if in defeat, but he smiled at her as he walked away. Somehow she felt as though he knew he had won, and she most definitely knew she had lost something precious in that moment.

PART TWO

One day when Samson was in Timnah, one of the Philistine women caught his eye. When he returned home, he told his father and mother, "A young Philistine woman in Timnah caught my eye. I want to marry her. Get her for me."

His father and mother objected. "Isn't there even one woman in our tribe or among all the Israelites you could marry?" they asked. "Why must you go to the pagan Philistines to find a wife?"

But Samson told his father, "Get her for me! She looks good to me." His father and mother didn't realize the LORD was at work in this, creating an opportunity to work against the Philistines, who ruled over Israel at that time.

—Judges 14:1–4 (NLT)

CHAPTER SIX

Within the month, Samson moved to live in Mahaneh-dan, a small town between the larger towns of Zorah and Eshtaol. Raya mourned his going with each empty day she remained with Manoah in Zorah.

"We can't follow him, Raya," Manoah had said the night after the grape harvest when Samson had broken the news to his father. "I am the firstborn of my father's house. This land is my inheritance, something I had hoped to pass to Samson when I am gone. I will not give it up to Elead or Ariel just to follow the whims of a youth who does not yet know his own mind."

"The men of Israel seem to think he knows his mind or they wouldn't come to him for advice," Raya shot back. "Even you have seen the Spirit of God moving in him, giving him wisdom beyond his years. And he invited us to live with him. Without a wife, how will he care for himself?"

She'd used every argument she could find to convince him, but now as she stood in the field behind their house, looking toward Mahaneh-dan, she knew the futility of her words. Yet her heart still longed to go to her son. The distance was not so far that he could not come home for meals if he wanted to. But he had remained away for several months now, and Manoah refused to discuss the matter any further.

"You are missing him," Talia said, coming up behind her. She touched Raya's shoulder then placed her arm around her.

Raya returned the half hug and then faced east again. "I do. Every day. If only Manoah would have allowed us to go with him." She faced her sister-in-law. "Who is feeding him? How is he faring? He hasn't even come home to talk to us."

Talia linked her arm through Raya's and they both turned, as Talia urged Raya to walk with her. "It will do us good to get away from the house," she said.

Raya followed as Talia turned the corner of the property and they circled the house that spread wide across the open fields. Gardens laced the terraced hills nearby and trees swayed in and around Manoah's property. "It is good land here," Talia said as they stopped near one of the terraces. "Samson will see that in time, Raya. He is just feeling the strength of his manhood and wants to live his life without restrictions. I fear that the Nazirite vow has caused him to seek freedom in other ways."

Raya stepped back to face Talia, crossing her arms over her chest. "I did not choose this life for him, no matter what anyone thinks. An angel of the Lord called Samson to be a Nazirite before his birth. The very fact that I even bore a son at all should show the world that I did not make this up to try to control my son."

Talia tilted her head and met Raya's gaze. "Raya, I believe you. I've watched Samson, and it is clear that God is with him. Even this move seems to be something God designed for him to do, though it breaks your heart to see it." She touched Raya's crossed arms. "Please know that your family understands and supports all of you. We will gladly welcome Samson back the moment he realizes that he misses us. But we cannot make him do what he will not do. If God is leading him, as you have always known He would, then who are we to stop God?"

Raya stared at Talia, noting the concern in her dark eyes and the lines drawn across her brow. She let her hands rest against her sides. "You are right, of course. God has been Samson's teacher all along. He gave him life and He called him to lead us against the Philistines. How He plans to do that, I do not know. But I suppose it is time that I learn to trust God with my son." Her shoulders sagged, her emotions bereft, defeated.

"It is not easy," Talia said, her tone gentle. "It is not easy to watch our boys grow up, marry, and bring girls that bicker into our home either. I fear we should have picked more compatible mates for our sons—at least women who liked each other. I feel like Rebekah, who found Esau's wives a constant irritant to her and Isaac." She laughed lightly, as though to cover her honest angst.

"I imagine having more than one child would give you cause to face such struggles. There is nothing you can say to make the girls get along?" Raya bent down to pick a ripe cucumber, then knelt, and Talia joined her as they both realized that this row of vegetables was ripe for picking. "We should have brought a basket."

"We can put them in our scarves."

They worked in silence a moment, until Raya glanced Talia's way. "I am sorry to be so unhappy around the family these days. It is my grief of losing him that awakens me each morn." Raya's face flushed hot with the admission. "That is, I miss him, and I grieve that he no longer needs me. And I fear I take it out on everyone who still does need me."

Talia smiled. "I could use your help to keep the girls from tearing at each other. And when Samson finds a wife and brings her home, I will do the same for you."

They both laughed, and Raya could not stop herself from being uplifted in Talia's presence. "I'm not sure our home is big enough to house Samson and a bride who would have him. He can be a force to reckon with, and if he chooses a wife who is like him..." She let the words linger.

What kind of woman would her son find acceptable? Had he asked his father to seek a wife for him? If he had, Manoah had not shared that information with her, and she should have the right to help him choose. By now they should have already started quietly gathering information on the kind of bride Samson would find compatible. And on the girl who would appreciate him.

But in that moment, Raya realized that Samson had said nothing of wanting a wife or asking her for help in finding one. She must ask Manoah if Samson had mentioned such a thing to him. Samson would not be so brash as to seek a woman on his own. He knew their customs and the importance of finding a wife who would share in his Nazirite vows, allowing him to do the work of God without tempting him to break God's trust.

Of course he did. Samson might be strong and stubborn, but he would obey their God. He was judging men of Israel according to the laws of God. He would not break them in such an important matter.

Would he?

Several months later, Raya looked up from her weaving at the sound of loud voices coming from the sitting room. She stopped the shuttle and hurried to see what was causing the commotion.

"Samson!" He stood, his bearing filling the room. Her sisters-in-law and nephews' wives stood about, mouths agape.

"Imma!" He strode toward her and lifted her off her feet in a hug she had missed for far too long.

"You are home, my son!" She leaned against him for a brief moment until he set her back on her feet.

"Yes. For a time." His smile warmed her, and her heart felt suddenly lighter. "Is my father at home? I did not see him at the town gate."

Raya looked up into Samson's eyes, searching them. "He went with your cousins and your uncle Elead to care for the sheep today. The Philistines have been raiding the flocks of the shepherds, and some from Timnah have come more often into our land. Your father has gone to help defend the flocks."

Samson's expression changed ever so slightly, his heavy brows drawn into a frown, yet her words seemed to have surprised him. "I have been to Timnah. I heard nothing of this."

Her eyes widened as she held his gaze. "You've been to Timnah? Why would you visit the enemy's city?" Her heartbeat quickened at the look he gave her, as if he fought conflicting emotions—both defensive of his reason for going and ashamed of going in the first place. *Please, Adonai, let it be the latter. Don't let me hear that he has done something of which You would not approve.*

"I had business there," he said, though his gaze skipped beyond hers. "How soon will my father return? What pasture are they in? I will go and find him." He turned but stopped as he reached the door.

"Won't you simply wait with me for him here, my son?" She desperately longed for him to stay, but his hand was already on the latch.

"What pasture?" His expression no longer seemed conflicted.

"I'm not sure. The south one, I think, but you know they move about often." She spoke but wondered if he heard beyond her first words, for he opened the door then and was gone before she could say more.

Her knees felt as though they would not hold her, and she couldn't decide whether to sink onto one of the cushions in the sitting room or return to her room and weep in private. For his actions, his dismissal of her concerns, his whole demeanor told her what she had fought against for months.

He had changed. Far too much. And not for the better.

Later that evening, once Raya had regained her determination and the shock of Samson's attitudes had dimmed, she helped prepare the meal and welcomed Manoah and Samson along with the rest of the men.

At the meal's end, Samson beckoned Manoah and Raya into their private rooms. They stood, watching him, until he motioned for them to sit. He sat before they did, and still Raya wanted to stand and block the door should he try to leave again.

"What is troubling you, Son?" Manoah asked, once Raya finally perched on the edge of a cushion.

"A young Philistine woman in Timnah caught my eye. I want to marry her. Get her for me." Samson's words held force, though his attempt to charm them with his famous smile remained.

Raya's heart sank as she rolled his request around in her mind, but no words would come to protest. How could they stop him when she could tell his mind was so set?

"Isn't there even one woman in our tribe or among all the Israelites you could marry?" Manoah asked, stirring her out of her stunned stupor.

"Yes," she agreed. "Why must you go to the pagan Philistines to find a wife?"

Samson looked at them, his dark eyes growing hard, his expression more determined than she had ever seen in him. Who was this man sitting before them? Certainly not the son she had raised!

"Get her for me!" His tone demanded and his fists clenched as he spoke. "She looks good to me."

"You would marry a woman—a foreign woman—on looks alone? What of your vow? What of our traditions? What of the law of our God?" Manoah had rarely spoken so harshly, but Raya silently agreed with him, her mind begging Samson to listen to reason.

"I've made up my mind, Abba. Do not deny me." There was no request in his tone, no attempt at reason.

Manoah lowered his head, holding it in his hands as if he had no strength to look his son in the eye.

"You would hurt us in this way, my son?" Raya gentled her tone, hoping it might have some effect on him.

"I do not mean it to hurt you, Imma," he said, looking at her with the first kindness she had seen in him since he'd barged into the house earlier that day. "But I want Dareen. Yes, she is a Philistine, but she loves me, and she appeals to me." He stood. "How soon will you go with me to make the arrangements?"

Silence followed the question, and Raya watched her son stand and begin to pace the small room. He could not marry the girl without them securing the bride price and agreeing to the contract. He knew that. But he acted as though they had no choice.

Did they have a choice?

She looked at Manoah, who had finally lifted his head, longing to tell him to refuse their son this foolishness, but Manoah did not look her way. "We will go with you at week's end. I need to find someone to take my place with your uncles and cousins in the fields."

"Week's end then. Good." He turned on his heel and left the room without a word of gratitude.

Raya's heart ached, the shock returning. She felt as though Samson had punched her in the belly, this beloved child who was once cradled there. "Why did you agree?" she finally asked her husband when she found her voice.

"Because I had no way to reason with him. I could not tell whether the Spirit of God was on him for him to be so demanding or whether he is simply following his own selfish ends. Either way, what was I to do? Deny him? He would only go and find another woman of whom we don't approve." He looked at her then. "He does not seek our approval, Raya. He only wants us to obey him."

The thought nearly took her breath. Ludicrous to think a child's parents should obey their child. He was breaking every law of God with regard to honoring parents. How could he think he would be pleasing to God if he so dishonored them?

But she did not say so. Manoah had already agreed to go, and there was nothing she could do but follow.

CHAPTER SEVEN

At week's end, Samson paced outside of his parents' door, his impatience growing with every step. They didn't want to go and do as he asked. He knew that. Had always known it even before he saw Dareen and determined to have her. But what his parents wanted ceased to matter to him once he entered Timnah and saw the enemy his parents had warned him about all of his life.

He had never seen anyone as beautiful as Dareen, not in any part of Israel. And a man had needs. Surely his parents knew that. And if he lived among the enemy, what better way to learn their secrets? He should have mentioned this idea to his parents to better convince them, but he doubted anything would have caused them to embrace his marriage to a Philistine. He'd been able to persuade them of smaller things all of his life, but this… He simply could not tell them everything that was on his heart or filled his mind.

His parents had so rarely denied him. The vow seemed to be the only thing they cared about or cared that he obeyed. So as long as he didn't break the vow, he still honored them. Eventually, they would see that his way was wise.

The door opened in the midst of his pacing and he smiled as his parents emerged, dressed in their finest clothes, his father carrying his staff in hand.

"At last you are ready," Samson said, giving them a slight scowl. "I feared the day would pass before we were off. Come. We have a long walk if we are going to get there and back by nightfall." He turned and started walking away from them, taking the path that led to Philistine territory, fully expecting them to follow.

His long strides moved him many paces ahead of them, and when he glanced back he noted that they did not walk with the speed he wanted. But they were older now, and perhaps he should take pity on them and slow his pace to match theirs.

He did so, though he inwardly chafed. "You will like Dareen, Imma," he said, attempting to ease the tension and bring peace to their furrowed brows. "Her parents are kind and they will welcome you." Though he did not know that for certain.

"What is her father's name?" his father asked. "It would help if we knew more about her and her family."

Samson smiled. This was a subject of which he knew little, but he did know their names. He should have spent more time getting to know all of her family and friends in greater detail, but there was still time. He would be married for many years, and Dareen liked to entertain guests. Samson envisioned a life of celebration. And where the wine flowed, men said more than they should. There would be plenty of opportunities for him to learn their secrets.

"Did you hear me, Son?"

His father's question brought him up short. How long had his thoughts taken him elsewhere? "Yes. I'm sorry, Abba. Your question caused me to think." He ran a hand down his long beard, something Dareen complained about but seemed to accept the one time he had kissed her—something he would not tell his parents.

"Her father is Wasim. Her mother is Adiya. Her little sister is Mirna. Her father is well known in Timnah, and the family is well off. It is a good match." Samson glanced at his father for his reaction.

"What work does her father do?" his mother asked. "Are they shepherds? Farmers?"

Samson's face grew warm at her scrutiny. "I'm not exactly sure, but if you ask them, I know they will tell you." He should have gathered more information before speaking to Dareen, something his parents would not have allowed before a betrothal. If he'd sought a woman of Israel, they would have kept him from her until they could secure the terms of the marriage.

"So you know very little about this girl or her family," his father said, his tone flat, not accusing, not accepting.

"Not yet, Abba." He suddenly felt the need to walk faster whether they could keep up or not. "We can talk more when we get there. It is important that we get there, so please come quickly." He moved ahead then, his frustration mounting. Why should it matter what the girl's father did to earn his wages or where they lived or what they thought or did with their time? He cared only for Dareen, for her beauty, for what he would do once they were finally alone and wed. Would that he could take her now, but he had a healthy fear of breaking God's law.

He quickened his pace, putting even more distance between them, feeling the struggle of hurting his parents and fulfilling his overwhelming need. Was he already breaking God's law by wanting to marry a Philistine? But no one in Israel matched Dareen in beauty. And hadn't God given the idea to him in the first place? Surely He had, though Samson could not stop the doubt that lingered. The last thing he needed was for his mother to find him a girl who obeyed every law but was impossible to look upon with pleasure.

He was pondering that and other conflicting thoughts when he suddenly realized that his parents were not even within his sight now. He neared the grapevines that led into Timnah, when out of the corner of his eye he saw swift movement. Before he could turn his head, a lion pounced on his back, its deep claws gripping his shoulders.

He roared back, tossing the animal to the ground, whirled about, and grabbed the lion by its bared jaws. In an instant, he felt powerful strength move through him and he ripped the jaws of the lion apart, blood spurting over his hands. Heart pounding, sweat beading his brow, he carried the dead body of the cat into the vineyards and tossed it there, off the road.

He paused to look. The cat was definitely motionless. Where had it come from? He'd never seen a wild cat in the daytime on this road. He breathed deeply, energized by the attack yet suddenly concerned that killing the animal had broken his Nazirite vow. He had touched the dead.

Moments later, the scent of the ripening grapes from the vineyard where he stood wafted to him, and he sniffed, inhaling the aroma he had never been allowed to taste. The sweet smell held a headiness he was not used to, and he looked at a large cluster hanging from a vine.

Would it really hurt for him to touch the skins? To taste one grape? Yet guilt from killing the cat suddenly filled him, and he knew he dared not break another of his vows. His mother's constant reminders filled his mind, and he turned quickly away and walked back to the road lest his parents discover him among the vines. He bent down and scooped up some dirt to rub the blood from his hands. He would wash off the dirt at the well outside of Timnah. His parents need never know.

He continued walking, though his gait slowed and a shiver worked through him as he realized how close he had come to breaking one of the most important vows of his birth. He glanced behind him and saw that his parents were at last in view. He stopped and waited for them to catch up to him.

"I need to wash before I take you to her home," he said, showing them his dirty hands.

His mother looked at him. "However did you get them so dirty, my son?" Skepticism filled her tired gaze.

"I tripped on a root and caught my fall with my palms. It will only take a moment to stop at the well to wash." The lie tasted bitter, but if they knew he had killed a lion, they would know he had broken part of his vow by touching a dead thing.

Curse the vow! And yet…no. The vow was good. The Spirit of God had given him strength. Still, he was weary of all of the restrictions, but he kept those thoughts to himself. He had gotten his parents this far. If they would go through with the agreement, everything would work itself out.

Raya followed Manoah into the Philistine house, her heart pounding at the very thought of being in enemy territory. She nodded and smiled and accepted the greeting of Dareen's parents, then followed Dareen and her mother and sister into the cooking area while the men met to discuss the betrothal agreement.

"I thought we would make raisin cakes, and the grapes are ripe and sweet so the wine for the wedding will be the best yet. We have never had such a harvest." Adiya spoke as though the food she planned for the betrothal feast would cause them no consternation. Had Samson told them nothing of his vow?

"Samson does not eat grapes or raisins or drink wine," she said, once Adiya finished the list of foods she had begun to prepare.

Dareen gave Raya a quizzical look. "He doesn't? He has never found anything wrong with the food we eat in the past."

How often had her son visited these people? How often had he stayed in Timnah? Did he eat their foods, forbidden to Israel, as well?

Raya told herself to stay calm. Just because Samson might not have disagreed with their diet didn't mean he had participated in it. "So he has eaten these things with you?" she asked, showing her surprise. "He has been a Nazirite from his birth and has never tasted these things." Until now? Her heart hurt to ask, but she had to know. She waited to hear their response.

Dareen's mouth dipped in a slight frown. "He has never minded that we eat them, but now that you say so, perhaps he hasn't actually partaken himself. I do not remember."

"You have no objection to us serving these things tonight, do you?" Adiyah asked, also frowning.

Raya felt cornered and wished for the hundredth time that Samson had not put them in this position. "This is your home," she said at last. "We are your guests. If you wish to serve these things, please do so, but also know that our God does not allow us to eat certain foods. I pray you will not be offended if we do not partake of them all."

Adiya searched Raya's face, her expression still one of disapproval, but at last she nodded. "I would not ask you to break the law of your god. We will serve enough food to please all of us." She turned to Mirna. "Gather some pistachios and let us make a sweet that does not include grapes or raisins."

"Yes, Imma." The younger girl left the area in a rush to do as she was told. Would that Samson had been as obedient as a child. But perhaps girls listened better than boys did.

"It shouldn't take the men long to come to acceptable terms," Adiya said. "If we all work together, the food will be ready by the time the guests arrive. Though as our guest, I do not expect you to help, Raya."

"I am happy to help. It is better than to sit with the men and have nothing to occupy my hands." Though if the truth were spoken, she would not be here at all. She held back a sigh and smiled. "Thank you for including me."

Dareen's mother nodded and bustled about the area, handing vegetables to Raya to wash and chop and lentils to Dareen to sort and boil, and sent servants to watch the pig roasting over a spit in the courtyard. The thought of the pig turned Raya's stomach, and she silently begged Adonai to forgive them for this decision and prayed they would not be adding the pig to other food, so they could avoid eating it.

"We have a lamb preparing as well," Adiya said, as if in answer to her prayer.

"Thank you." Raya glanced at the ceiling, grateful that God could hear past the stone and wooden structures of men. Now all they had to do was to survive this day and go home and wait for the wedding, however long from now that would be.

CHAPTER EIGHT

Six Months Later

The day of the wedding arrived, and Raya woke early to prepare as she had planned. The new coat she had woven for Samson she'd completed early and in her frantic need to occupy her mind, she'd made new robes for Manoah and herself as well. She dared not allow her family to appear before the detested Philistines looking as though they were the poor shepherds they were.

She glanced now at her reflection in the bronze mirror. She would not use kohl or other dyes or colorings for her face, despite Samson's desire she do so. Instead, she took some of the precious oils of balsam and frankincense and moistened the skin along her face and neck. They brought a soft glow to cover the wan tint she had acquired of late. She had not taken her daily walks in the sunshine as often as she used to, preferring to remain hidden away from those who might say harsh words against her for her son's choice of a bride and his parents' inability to deny him.

And what could she say in their defense? She had doted on her only child all of his life, with only one request—that he keep the vow the angel of the Lord had placed on them. But to marry a Philistine? She had heard the whispers of Karmela and Talia's daughters-in-law. Even Talia had wondered if they could do anything to stop the marriage, but the message still came to Raya loud and clear. *How could you let your son marry a Philistine?* And indeed, how was it possible that they had not had the fortitude to say no to their son? Samson had been so utterly persuasive. Surely their family and friends knew how he was, how insistent, even demanding he could be.

But they had also seen the disrespect he showed his parents simply by asking them to seek a foreign bride for him. It dishonored their wishes, but Samson seemed not to notice or care. He was interested in what he wanted and only that, no matter how many times since the betrothal Manoah and she had pleaded with him to reconsider.

Samson had finally left their home again and sought refuge in Mahaneh-dan as he had before. He'd returned home a week ago to make sure all was ready for this day. No doubt he would be knocking on their door before the sun was barely above the horizon.

A knock did come as she was putting the cap on the jar of scented oil. She straightened, picked up the sack with their change of clothes for the seven days they would be away, and smoothed her robe. Manoah had already dressed and gone to check on the goat he intended to take as a gift for the bride's family.

Raya opened the door, surprised that the knock came from within the house, expecting to see Samson, when she saw Talia standing there with a spray of flowers in hand.

"I thought you might like to offer these to the bride's mother," she said, smiling in her usual kind way. "You look lovely, Raya."

"I look tired and worn," she said, her voice low, but her mind felt as sluggish as the blood slowly moving through her veins. When had she begun to feel so old?

Talia took her arm and nudged her outside, where they could escape those who might be listening. No sign of Samson pacing yet, and Raya breathed a sigh, grateful for the moment's reprieve. "You are nervous and sad, Raya. And in the six months since this agreement was made, I have not heard you sing. I know you grieve. And it is not wrong that you feel grief over your son's choice." Talia touched her shoulder in a comforting gesture. "You raised him well, and he knows the truth. He knows what God requires of him, but this decision to marry a Philistine… There was nothing you could do to stop this. You know better than the rest of us what it is like when his mind is made up."

Raya nodded, fighting the urge to allow tears to turn her eyes red. "He is a good son," she said, never able to stop defending him.

"Of course he is." Talia's fierce tone warmed her.

"But a stubborn one. And proud." Raya whispered the words lest someone hear. She glanced about. Still no sign of Manoah or Samson. Perhaps they were at the other door, expecting her to exit around the corner of the house.

"God will deal with those things," Talia said softly. "We do our best as mothers. And if we believe that our God is true, then we know we can trust Him to finish what He began. We raise the child, but He makes the man into what He wants him to be."

Raya swallowed the lump in her throat. Karmela did not believe as they did, yet her children followed the law to this day. None had given her cause for grief, and yet perhaps they followed as their mother did—because that was the way of the household. Talia and Elead believed as Manoah and Raya did and they both struggled with their children, only in different ways. It made no sense, but Raya could not think of that now.

"He's going to marry the girl today, like it or not," Raya said at last. "And we will support him the best way we can. I wish the family could join us." She heard the wistfulness in her tone, but she knew she could never ask it of them. "But I know that you do from afar."

"Elead feels it safer to guard the flocks and stay home rather than expose the entire family to the Philistines. If the time comes that Samson can raise an army against them and calls us to war, then I'm sure our sons will join him. And of course, we can't all stay away seven days and leave the animals alone." Talia gave Raya a gentle hug. "Now, let us see if we can find your men. You don't want to be late for your son's wedding!"

I don't want to go at all. But she did not say so. "No. We cannot be late. Manoah still has a few things to work out with Dareen's father."

"Will Samson bring her to live among us?" Talia asked almost as a last thought as they neared the corner of the house.

Raya stopped, facing her sister-in-law. "I do not think that ever crossed his mind. He has not built a room for her, and he talks often of going to her rather than going to get her."

Talia nodded. Was that relief in her gaze? But Raya knew the family would find it hard to welcome a Philistine into their home. "Perhaps in time things will change."

"Perhaps." They turned the corner and there Manoah and Samson waited with the goat tied to a rope.

"There you are," Samson said, seeming to try to curb the frustration she heard in his tone. "Can we go now?"

"I am ready," Raya said. She hugged Talia one more time, took the spray of flowers from her, and then joined her men. This was going to be a long day.

Samson walked with them the first third of the way, but Raya could feel the anxious tension in his step until at last he moved ahead of them as he had the last time. Raya opened her mouth, about to ask him to slow down, when she felt Manoah's hand on her arm. "Let him go," he said, his expression carrying defeat.

"He is anxious to be with Dareen." She knew that, but neither she nor Manoah had any desire to rush into Timnah.

"Yes. And to start a life of wild living with uncircumcised foreigners who oppress our people. Honestly, Raya, I cannot understand why there is no reasoning with him. It is as though I say something and he hears something else. Every attempt ends in his silence or defiance."

Raya slipped her arm through her husband's. "I know. Perhaps I coddled him too much as a child. He was our only son, only child, and I could deny him little since the vow demanded so much of him."

"I was no better. Now and then I could reprimand him, but when we were forced to deny him what God required of him alone, I couldn't bear to not give in to the things he *could* do." Manoah tugged on the goat's rope, coaxing it to stay alongside them.

"We did our best," Raya said, hoping to comfort him. Comfort *herself,* if she admitted the truth. "Perhaps one day he will come to his senses."

"And do what? Divorce her? Would that be better?" Manoah's look held the pain of one who struggles.

"Considering he is marrying a foreigner who does not share the knowledge of our God, I think so." Raya shook her head. "I don't know enough of the law to know what Adonai would want of him. He seems to be living a life different from the rest of us."

"We must pray more for him, Raya. He will fall hard if we do not. I sense it." Manoah's words made Raya's heart nearly stop.

"I pray for him continually." Yet nothing changed. Did God hear her cries for her son? He had heard once when He at last gave her Samson, but now... If he was chosen of God, why was he disobedient to God's law?

The question lingered as they caught up to Samson, who seemed to have waited for them. He licked something from his fingers and strode toward them, smiling.

"I found some honey," he said, offering them a taste. "It will give us strength for the long day ahead." His look held pleading.

Raya broke off a piece of the dripping honeycomb and quickly plopped it into her mouth lest it land on her robe. Manoah did the same, each licking their fingers. Samson offered them more, and Raya took one smaller piece.

"It is very good," Raya said, feeling her spirits lifting with the fresh sweetness. "Where did you get it?" She glanced about but saw no sign of bees or a hive hanging from a tree.

"Off the road a bit," he said, turning to walk slightly ahead of them again. "It was a fortunate find."

"Yes," Manoah said, though Raya heard the concern, even skepticism in his tone. Was their son keeping a secret from them?

She licked the last of the honey from her fingers and picked up some dirt to remove the sticky feeling from her hand. Had Samson found honey the last time they came this way and covered his hands in dirt so they wouldn't know? But why keep honey a secret when this time he shared it with them?

When Samson was out of sight, she leaned closer to her husband. "I think there is something Samson is not telling us."

Manoah met her gaze. "I think there is a lot Samson has not told us in years. Beginning with his visits to Timnah. Where else has he been and what else has he done in the years he has chosen to live away from us? Do you honestly think this marriage is his first attempt to break his vows?" Hurt laced his tone, even as he glanced ahead to make sure they were out of Samson's earshot.

"No," she said at last. "I do not think it is the first time. He has chafed at the vow since he could walk." It hurt to remember, for with it came too many times when they fought over his life's restrictions. "But I think God will use him regardless. Why else would he have been born? God will use him whether he knows it or not."

"If he accepted his role, his life would be better," Manoah said, despite his nod of agreement.

"Yes, but either way we know he is in God's hands." She had to believe that. It had been true since his birth. Surely it would be true all of his life. She could only hope that one day he would accept the God who gave him the vow and the power to carry out His work instead of fighting against the very God who made him in the first place.

CHAPTER NINE

Dareen's father's house came into view, and Raya's heart sank upon hearing the celebratory sounds coming from within. She discreetly wiped the moisture still on her hands from washing them at the well and carried the spray of flowers toward the door, her heart thumping too fast. Why was she so nervous? But something about this place did not bring her peace.

Manoah left her side and guided the goat toward the outbuilding where Dareen's father and the other men of the town were assembling for prewedding festivities. Samson had followed his father, his step light and laughter bursting from his lips. Oh that she could share in that laughter. If only he were about to wed a virgin in Israel. But none of that could be helped now.

Raya swallowed and willed herself not to tremble. She should be happy for her son, as he was happy for himself. But she could not bring herself to feel in any way good about this moment. Before she could think of what to do next, however, the door opened, and Adiya welcomed her.

"Raya, come in, come in!" She moved aside and gestured with her arm in a wide arc. "Join us." She took the flowers from Raya's hand and thanked her, smiling. "We are gathering the women here, while Wasim and the others send for the young men to be Samson's companions. Once they all arrive, the feasting and celebrating can begin!"

Raya smiled and nodded, wondering if Adiya had already drunk too much wine, for it was early in the day and yet Adiya's speech held a slight slur and there was a giddy tone in her voice. Raya glanced around, seeing a number of older women she did not recognize all seated on plush cushions, holding cups of wine—or was it simply water?—in their hands.

Talk ceased among them as she approached and sat where Adiya had led her. "Greetings," she said, smiling at each one, hoping her angst was well hidden behind her expression.

"Welcome our groom's mother," Adiya said to her friends. She turned to Raya. "Dareen and her sister are with the younger women in their rooms. We will not come together, but Wasim and I will each host our own festivities. The younger girls will join us soon."

Raya's eyes widened, but she simply nodded. This was not the custom of her people. Would they have separate wedding celebrations? When would the bride and groom come together? Was there no blessing of the couple, no bridegroom's tent? But she did not ask.

As the afternoon wore on, Raya said little as she observed a beautiful yet spoiled Dareen enter the room, her mother and the other women flattering her with constant praises. In the distance, she could hear the men laughing and growing louder, probably most thoroughly drunk by now. Was Samson keeping his vow? Would Manoah be able to coax him or at least remind him to do so?

Raya had never felt so lost and out of place, and she wished for the hundredth time that she could begin the walk toward home. But this grand feast would last seven days, and the only respite she would get was when she could find a place to sleep, hopefully with her husband, away from the cursed Philistines.

This week could not end soon enough.

Samson stood in the center of the large building, pleased with the thirty young men his bride's parents had chosen for him to toy with during the wedding feast. He waved away the cup of wine offered to him and smiled at the servant, who stood dumbfounded at his rejection of the drink. To distract those watching, he jumped down from the groom's throne and stood in the center of the room.

"Let me tell you a riddle," he called out, drawing the attention of each of the thirty young men. The older men watched from the sidelines, but everyone knew this game was for his companions.

"If you solve my riddle during these seven days of the celebration, I will give you thirty fine linen robes and thirty sets of festive clothing. But if you can't solve it, then you must give me thirty fine linen robes and thirty sets of festive clothing."

Laughter followed his comment, and the young men exchanged looks as if they thought it all a great joke. "All right," they agreed, "let's hear your riddle."

Samson avoided his father's gaze, which he could nearly feel pointed his way. He had not told his parents about the lion or that the honey he'd given them had come from the lion's carcass. Or that he had entered a vineyard and nearly broken his vow regarding grapes. Better to keep them innocent of his choices and actions as much as he could. His father would not be able to understand his riddle any more than the men would, but Samson could live with that. It would work to his father's advantage and keep him blameless should the young men grow angry when Samson won the bet.

He hid a smile at his thoughts, for he knew he could best all of them in this. At last he lifted a hand and spoke.

"Out of the one who eats came something to eat; out of the strong came something sweet."

The men stared at him then began to whisper among themselves. Samson called out, "Seven days. Surely you can figure it out by then." He smiled and returned to the seat they had set aside for him.

His father, who sat near him as the second most honored guest, leaned close to his ear. "That is quite a riddle you have posed. I assume you have come across something that put the idea in your mind."

Samson felt his face flush as he turned to meet his father's gaze. "Yes, you are quite right. I have a very logical answer for my riddle, though they will never figure it out." He kept his voice low and laughter hidden, as he did not wish to mock his companions, who were there to help him celebrate. This was, after all, a festive day.

As evening came and the sun blazed its brilliant farewell on the western horizon, the young men had all fallen asleep in various places about the room, too drunk to return to their homes for the night and return to the feast the following evening.

Samson's father slipped away to find his mother and sleep in the guest room prepared for them, while Samson went to find Dareen. She was waiting for him at the entrance to the suite of rooms her parents had decorated in subtle colors and low lights placed near the large plush bed. Her father's position as owner of vast vineyards had afforded him great wealth, and they did not seem to mind pouring it out on their firstborn child.

Dareen beckoned him forward and took his hand, leading him into the privacy of the scented rooms. He shut the door and latched it, then went to her, hungry for her. He lifted her with ease among the soft linens of the cushioned bed, and wasted no time removing every garment she had likely taken much time in placing over her stunning body. But Samson had little use for the beautiful clothing or jewels she wore. He was consumed with her from her head to her toes. And before the night ended, he had taken every part of her that was once hers alone and made it his.

"Samson has posed a riddle to the young men of the Philistines," Manoah told Raya that first night as they lay beside each other in the room Dareen's parents had given for their use. "I fear he is purposely toying with them and it will not end well."

"For him or for them?" she asked, nestling into the crook of his arm, grateful for the chance to be out of her good clothes.

"For them and for him. He plays with things he does not understand." Manoah could not stifle a yawn, but she heard the fear in his voice.

"What did he pose to them?"

"He told them a riddle, and if they can't solve it during the wedding week, they will owe him thirty suits of clothes. That's one robe and tunic per young man. Not a hefty price for men of their standing, but these men will not want to be bested, no matter the cost." He raked a hand through his hair. "What is he thinking?"

"That he is smarter than they are," Raya said softly. It would do no good to be overheard through the walls. "You know that is his way."

Manoah grunted and rolled on his side. "He's asking for trouble."

Soft snoring soon followed, but Raya could not sleep. *Samson, Samson, what are you trying to do to us? To yourself?* And then her thoughts for her son turned to silent prayers for his safety. She had never had a good feeling about this situation and now that they were here, captive in a sense under a Philistine roof, she felt physically ill. These women would never accept her nor she them.

Even knowing there were only six more days did nothing to calm her or lessen her fear. She would lose him for good if he didn't use caution. And yet the memory of the angel of the

Lord rose in her thoughts, making her wonder if Samson was born for caution or for this—whatever *this* turned out to be.

Four days passed, and still the young men could not figure out Samson's riddle. Raya listened to the whispers of the older women, mothers of some of the young men, concern lining their brows, but when she drew near, they looked away, avoiding her.

Dareen had not shown her face that morning, but by late afternoon, she burst into the room weeping, calling for Samson. He came to her and drew her aside, near where Raya happened to be standing, having just come from the cooking rooms.

"You don't love me; you hate me!" Dareen shouted, making Samson's attempts at privacy null. "You have given my people a riddle, but you haven't told me the answer."

"I haven't even given the answer to my father or mother," Samson said, his voice low. "Why should I tell you?"

"Because they told me they would burn down my father's house with me in it if you don't tell me. They said, 'Did you invite us to this party just to make us poor?'" Weeping followed the remark, and Raya's heart beat hard at the violence of the threat. She shouldn't be surprised. Philistines could be brutal. Hadn't they oppressed the people of Israel for years? But to burn Dareen alive? Her whole body grew weak at the thought.

"They are idle threats, Dareen," Samson said, wooing her with his familiar charm. "Do not listen to them. Think how rich we will be when they cannot answer the riddle! That's good for us, is it not?"

She grew silent a moment, and Raya strained to hear, but they moved away, Dareen to her rooms and Samson outside to join the young men.

Was it an idle threat? Or was Manoah right? Samson was playing a dangerous game. Three days remained for the men to guess the answer to Samson's riddle. Would Dareen let it go and trust Samson? Or would she continue to nag him? And if she nagged him, what good would that do? Nagging had never done her any good as his mother.

Raya released a breath, realizing she'd been holding it for too long. Three more days and they could leave. She moved to the door to walk outside, needing a break from the stifling house and its foreign, unfriendly women. *Please, Adonai, do not let my son be ruined by this woman.* Or by her people.

CHAPTER TEN

Raya woke early on the last day of the feast, relief filling her. Soon it would all be over and she could draw a deep breath again! The thought brought a smile to her lips, and though Manoah still slept at her side, she rose, quickly dressed, and went out into the gray predawn light. The area behind the house near the outbuilding held a well-worn path, and she took it, curious to see where the men had celebrated, then determined to walk in the fields before the household awoke and a final day of drunkenness began.

Today would be the day Samson would win or lose his bet with the younger men, and Raya's heart skipped a beat, fear suddenly rising within her. It had been impossible to ignore Dareen's weeping and the shouts coming from the room Samson shared with her on what should have been a happy occasion. No good could come of the arguments. Nagging Samson to tell her the answer would bring ruin upon Samson.

A shiver worked through Raya at the thought, even as her feet moved slowly closer to the outbuilding. Had Dareen been successful with Samson? The weeping had stopped in the middle of the night, which was actually the start of the seventh day, and brought a collective sigh to the household. But Raya worried.

She approached the wide door, large enough for an animal to pass through, and stopped at the sound of voices. The household had been drinking long after she and Manoah had gone to bed, and usually did not rise until the sun was halfway to the sky. Who was up at this hour of dawn?

"He told me the answer to his riddle." The voice was soft but without doubt belonged to Dareen.

Raya stepped closer but stayed to the side of the building and glanced about, hoping she was not seen.

"Tell us quickly." A young man spoke, his voice anxious, angry.

"What is sweeter than honey? What is stronger than a lion?" Dareen's tone held triumph, and Raya could imagine the proud tilt to the young woman's round chin and the slanted look in her dark eyes.

Laughter followed her words, and Raya glanced about again, fearing someone would come through the door and see her there. She should leave, but another man's voice stopped her.

"It is a good thing that you got him to tell you," he said, his pitch low and menacing. "We would not have liked to see your beautiful body burned alive."

More laughter followed the remark. Surely the girl would run away from such a threat. But as Raya moved away from the door, she heard Dareen's own laughter mingling with that of the men.

"You know you would rather taste and see this rather than destroy it." Raya dared not look to see of what she spoke, but her mind whirled with the possibilities. Had she been unfaithful to Samson already?

The fields beckoned her, and she felt her breath release in a whoosh as her feet sank into the softer grassy soil where wildflowers bloomed and trees waved their branches in the distance. Should she tell Samson what she had heard? Or let him find out tonight that he had lost the bet because of his unfaithful wife? Would he trust her again? Would the anger he would surely feel cause him to react against Dareen and her family and friends?

Oh, Adonai, what should I do? She and Manoah could leave before the riddle was brought up. She could feign illness, and they could leave Samson to decide what he would. But was that not abandoning him? How could a mother even think such thoughts? And yet she did not wish to be caught in the middle when he reacted to this news.

She walked on even as the sun began to whisk away the dew from the grasses. She must tell Manoah. He would know better than she what they should do. Though she had once held influence over Samson, it was obvious that his weakness lay with his wife, not his mother. No amount of begging or nagging on her part had changed his mind—it had just caused him to walk away. Whereas Dareen could control him with her tears.

"We can't leave him," Manoah said, once Raya told him what she had heard. "I cannot say that I understand the answer or why he would say something sweet could come from a lion, but obviously, he knows, and now the men know. We need to be here for him. Perhaps we can keep him from doing anything rash."

"When have we ever been able to keep him from doing what he is determined to do? He doesn't listen to us, Manoah." Raya lifted her hands in a defeated gesture, trying to make him see. She had decided on her long morning walk that she no longer wanted to be here.

"He may not listen, but he is our son. We stay." Manoah touched her shoulder. "It's only one more night, Raya. Please try to make the best of it."

But as night fell and the men and women gathered in the outbuilding one last time, Raya's whole body tensed as Samson again posed his riddle.

"So, tell me," he said, "out of the one who eats came something to eat; out of the strong came something sweet. What is your answer?"

The thirty young men stepped up to Samson where he sat on the groom's throne. One moved closer and lifted his hands, a smile on his face. "What is sweeter than honey?" he said. "What is stronger than a lion?"

Silence followed the remark, and Raya watched Samson's skin turn many shades of red, darkening the longer he sat looking over each man, meeting each gaze.

At last he spoke. "If you hadn't badgered my wife, you wouldn't have solved my riddle!"

"Yes, but we have solved it and you owe us thirty sets of clothing. Tell me, Samson," the bold one who stood as the leader said, mocking, "are you going to weave them, or do you happen to have them with you?" He laughed. "You didn't think you could lose and then rob us at a feast you didn't pay for, did you? Well, now you need to pay."

Samson stood, towering over the men, who all took a giant step back. "You want to be paid? Fine! Wait here and you will have your fine garments!" With that he turned toward the door, shoving past everyone, and hurried out of the building.

Raya and Manoah rose and quickly followed him.

"Where are you going, Son?" Manoah called at Samson's swiftly retreating back.

Samson stopped, whirled about. "Go home, Abba. You and Imma have no place here now. Go home where it is safe." He turned around again and half ran away from them.

Raya looked at Manoah, whose mouth remained open, as if he had been about to speak, then quickly shut it and took her arm. "He is right. Let us gather our things and go. Whatever he is about to do will not end well, as I predicted."

Raya simply nodded. She left him to enter the house and grabbed the sack with their nightclothes and ointments then slipped out the door before a servant or Dareen's family could see her. The rest of the people had remained in the outbuilding and Raya had no desire to ever see them again—including Dareen.

She met Manoah in the courtyard, his staff in hand, and began the long walk home, wondering what their son would do.

Samson moved down the path from Timnah to Ashkelon faster than a trotting mule. Fury drove him despite the growing darkness, and he clenched his fists in and out, cursing his bride and her friends under his breath with every step. Make a fool of him, would they? They would regret the day they had ever laid their eyes upon him or his parents!

Uncircumcised Philistines! He would give them their clothing. And take the lives of their people in the process. The determination grew along with his anger, and he sensed great strength pulsing through him with every beat of his heart. The three miles to Ashkelon took far less time than in the past when he had wandered through Philistine lands. He knew exactly where to find the men he sought and headed straight for the wealthy section of the city but not too close to the palace of the ruling Philistine lord.

Darkness shrouded the city as he slipped inside just before they closed the gates. He moved stealthily to the homes of the wealthy and crept into their houses, first one, then another, killing men in their sleep without so much as waking a wife or a child. He loaded his arms with their belongings and snuck out of the last house.

He should have brought a donkey with him to carry the load, for by the time he had all thirty sets of clothing, he had to tie them into a bundle in order to hoist them onto his back. Silence blanketed the city, a surprise to him, for he thought to find some of the men visiting the houses of ill repute or drinking together before going home. But the sun had set long ago, and it was as though God Himself had placed His blessing on His work and allowed him to take from the Philistines a small part of what they had taken from Israel.

The desire to smile or even laugh outright at his success and their loss filled him but he quashed it. First he must free himself from the confines of the city and be almost to Timnah before he would allow himself to celebrate.

The gate was locked and guards stood nearby, so he slipped into one of the side rooms, knocked out the guard standing there, and opened the smaller gate that was barred but allowed those few who had been delayed to enter once they passed the guard's inspection. He closed the door behind him, though it would no longer be latched until the guard awoke, and silently chuckled at his good fortune.

Surely God was with him.

He shifted the weight on his back and ducked his head, hurrying back toward Timnah. No doubt the guests would have left by now, though he had told them to wait. He would go to his father-in-law's home to see, but then he would find each man and toss the clothing in his face. Let them mock him then!

Darkness deepened and the stars exploded in the sky, while the moon guided his path. He trudged on, picking up his pace. He arrived at his wife's house, but the lights had been extinguished and no sound came from either the house or the outbuilding.

Anger turned to rage as he approached the outbuilding, dropped the clothes, and yanked open the door. Moonlight showed the men drunk and sleeping about the room. He should kill them all. The thought warred within him, but at last he lifted the clothes in his arms and took them about the room, dropping a set over the face of each man.

They sputtered and batted the robes and tunics away, but Samson did not turn to even glance behind him. When the last set of clothing landed on the last drunken Philistine, he marched out of the building and headed back toward the home of his father-in-law, where his wife should be waiting for him. But with each step, his pace slowed. How could she have betrayed him like that? He cared not for the Philistines he had killed, but she had humiliated him by sharing his confidence with the young men. She should have feared him more than them. He could turn around even now and kill them all with one blow!

Resentment and hurt swelled, and he suddenly could not go back. He feared his own strength and what he might do to her or her father for what had been done to him. At his own wedding. They should have gladly given him a gift of clothing. A wedding gift. Instead they had expected to be paid by him! For what? For showing up at his own marriage feast?

Ungrateful in-laws! Didn't they know who he was? What he could do to them all if God called him to do it?

He shifted direction and headed back toward his parents' home. He would return to Dareen another day but not this night. He could not face another moment of her nagging or look at her beautiful form and know that she had betrayed his trust.

He wasn't sure he could ever look at her again.

PART THREE

Later on, during the wheat harvest, Samson took a young goat as a present to his wife. He said, "I'm going into my wife's room to sleep with her," but her father wouldn't let him in.

"I truly thought you must hate her," her father explained, "so I gave her in marriage to your best man. But look, her younger sister is even more beautiful than she is. Marry her instead."

Samson said, "This time I cannot be blamed for everything I am going to do to you Philistines." Then he went out and caught 300 foxes. He tied their tails together in pairs, and he fastened a torch to each pair of tails. Then he lit the torches and let the foxes run through the grain fields of the Philistines. He burned all their grain to the ground, including the sheaves and the uncut grain. He also destroyed their vineyards and olive groves.

"Who did this?" the Philistines demanded.

"Samson," was the reply, "because his father-in-law from Timnah gave Samson's wife to be married to his best man." So the Philistines went and got the woman and her father and burned them to death.

"Because you did this," Samson vowed, "I won't rest until I take my revenge on you!" So he attacked the Philistines with great fury and killed many of them. Then he went to live in a cave in the rock of Etam.

—Judges 15:1–8 (NLT)

CHAPTER ELEVEN

Six Months Later

Raya walked to the courtyard where Karmela, Talia, and the younger girls had gathered to prepare the day's meals. "Greetings," she said, her heart lighter than it had been in months. Wheat harvest was upon them and with Samson home, his help would bring the crop in sooner than later, for he worked with the strength of two men, sometimes more. At least that was how it seemed to her, and she had never been gladder to have him back home these past six months.

"Raya, good day to you," Talia said, handing her a sack of grain to be ground.

Karmela nodded in her direction, already busy with the first batch of bread. "You have never been an early riser," Karmela said, her words holding less of their usual sting. With Samson home, nothing could upset Raya's peace, not even Karmela. Besides, Raya consoled herself, she had been up before dawn as she often was. She simply preferred time in the fields to pray before she joined the others, especially since Karmela seemed to love flaunting her control over the preparation of their food.

"Forgive me," Raya said, not knowing what else she could say. There was no pleasing Karmela, despite her many attempts.

"I was in the fields. The harvest has already begun, even before dawn had fully risen."

"Did you think you were going to cut the grain with the men?" This from one of the younger wives of Karmela's sons. The girls seemed to have picked up the same caustic tongue of their mother-in-law.

"Of course she didn't," Talia said, coming to her defense. "Raya is not needed here so early, so she walks and prays before she joins us. You cannot fault her for that."

"If I took that long to pray, we would never eat." Karmela's face darkened, but she would not meet either Talia's or Raya's gaze.

"I will come sooner next time then." Raya did not need to ruin this day when her son was home and the harvest would mean food for the coming year. This was a pleasant day, if she could keep it so.

"Do not trouble yourself. We do fine without you."

Raya stiffened at Karmela's disrespect. Despite the fact that Raya stood as the mother of the household with Adah's passing, Karmela had never accepted her place. And Raya had no desire to fight with her or to invite Manoah into her personal struggles.

"Karmela!" Talia rose up as if to fight to defend Raya. "You have said quite enough."

Karmela pressed her lips together and did not respond. Neither did she apologize, just continued to work in silence.

Raya's pleasant mood dipped, and she took up the grinding stone to drown out the awkward silence. She would finish her tasks here and go back to the fields. Someone had to take water to the men, and she would do it whether the women liked it or not. But she missed the days before Karmela's and Talia's daughters-in-law had moved in and brought hostile attitudes with them. Though Talia's girls had softened of late, Karmela seemed to encourage hostility against Raya.

The only question that constantly nagged her was why?

Raya searched her mind and came up empty. All she could think of was that perhaps they resented Samson and all of the extra work it took to help him keep his vow. When he lived away from them, the women seemed pleased, while Raya's heart hurt. Was that it? Did they resent her son? She glanced at Talia, who offered her a sympathetic smile.

Or was it the fact that she was not as pleasant to be near when Samson was gone, especially when he left no warning as to where he would be? Was her heart so tied up in her son's life that she could not be happy without him near?

She pondered the thought as she ground the wheat, not willing to probe deep enough to answer her own question.

"I'm going to Timnah," Samson announced later that evening before Manoah and Raya retired for bed. "I want to sleep with my wife."

They stood in the small sitting area in their part of the larger house, staring at their son. "We are in the middle of wheat harvest, my son. Can this not wait until it is over? We could use your strength and help. The work is getting to be too much for me without the younger men working beside us. Won't you stay until we finish?" Manoah lifted his hands toward Samson in supplication. His words carried the pleading tone Raya wanted to use.

"You have my cousins, Abba. There are many of them, and my uncles are younger than you are. They still have the strength to bring in a crop." Samson's voice carried no sympathy or understanding for his father's wishes.

"We could still use your help, Samson," Raya said softly. She met his gaze, struck by the intense desire in his eyes, something she'd only seen at his wedding feast. He missed Dareen, and apparently had at last lost his anger toward her.

"I will give you one more day," Samson said, offering them a guarded smile. "But then I'm going. And I'm taking a goat from the flock for my father-in-law. It would do no good to show up without bearing a gift."

"Thank you, Son." Manoah touched Samson's shoulder, and they bid him good night.

Raya looked into her husband's haggard face. "You are tired."

Manoah nodded. "I fear I do not have the vigor I once had. And my heart has grown weary of Samson's constant change of mind. He demands things of us without asking. He would just take a goat? The goats do not belong to him. Not yet. Not until my death. And why return to the Philistine wife six months after the wedding when he hadn't bothered to visit sooner? His ways make no sense to me, and honestly, Raya, he wears me out. He says one thing then does another. I never know whether I can believe him to keep his word."

"And yet he still judges Israel at the city gate, so he must have some good in his thinking." Why she always defended him troubled her. This was her husband, who looked as though he had aged three years in the past six months. Was he ill? Worry gnawed the pit of her stomach.

"Yes, yes, he seems capable of judging cases the men bring to him. But he seems incapable of honoring his parents' wishes. I wonder which one God honors more. Judging people is not one of the commandments. Honoring his parents is." He raked a hand through his hair and headed to his pallet. "I'm tired, Raya. Let us speak no more of our son. I have to be up early to harvest, and I have no idea whether Samson will actually join us or not." He removed his robe and sank onto the pallet, pulling the cloak over him for warmth.

Raya joined him, watching him as he closed his eyes in an attempt to sleep. How long would she have him? She could not lose Manoah. Samson would not take care of her if his father passed into Sheol. She would be alone at the mercy of Elead and the rest of Manoah's family. Even as the wife of the first-born, Raya held no rights to his property—only his son did. A son who right now could not be trusted.

Samson rose early the day after he'd helped a second time with the wheat harvest. They had gathered in most of the crop now, and his cousins could finish the work. He needed to see Dareen. Needed to be with her again. Why couldn't his father understand that?

He untied the goat he had chosen from the peg at the door of the pen and led it out, latching the gate that housed the others. His father would know he had left when he saw that the goat was gone. He walked the familiar path, his mind whirling with too many thoughts. Did God want him to sit at a city gate and judge Israel, or defeat Israel's enemies and restore the land to Israel alone?

Was his father unwell? Or were his pleas for Samson to stay home for reasons he did not explain? Did his mother know something about his father she had not told him? Why was she always upset to see him leave? To see her sad always troubled him, so he left early before either of them was up. He needed to get away. Six months away from his wife was too long, but his anger had taken that long to subside.

But now…now things would improve. He would forgive her and they would move away from her father's house and he would slowly begin to find ways to infiltrate her people and eventually, he would have his retribution. But not on Dareen. He would spare his wife. The rest of the Philistines, they would not fare so well after what he had suffered, what Israel had suffered at their hands.

He looked ahead, the house coming now into view. He coaxed the goat to move faster then finally picked it up and carried it to the door and knocked.

Rushing footsteps sounded from inside the house, loud enough to hear from where he stood outside the door. At last, Wasim opened it to him.

"Samson! What a surprise to see you." The man seemed nervous, unusual for him. And why was he inside the house instead of out inspecting his vineyards? But he did not ask.

He offered the goat to the man, who took it awkwardly from him, then set it on the ground and held the rope tied to its neck. "You bring a gift." Wasim acted strange, as though such a gesture was unexpected. A wary feeling crept up Samson's neck.

"I'm going into my wife's room to sleep with her," he said, taking a step forward.

But Wasim stood in his path, blocking the door. He swallowed, his Adam's apple visibly bobbing above his tunic. "I truly thought you must hate her," Wasim said, the words shaky rather than carrying his normal confidence. "So I gave her in marriage to your best man." He glanced behind him and back at Samson, then called Mirna to come to him. "But look," he hastily added, "her younger sister is even more beautiful than she is. Marry her instead."

Samson stared at the man as though he had lost his senses. He did not even glance at Mirna, who was practically still a child. Did the man think him mad? He gave Dareen to another? One of the men who had stood beside him at the wedding? He searched his mind, for he struggled to remember which one Wasim had set to be his best man. Samir. Yes, that was his name. But he could not recall his face, and he could not believe his father-in-law could do something so foolish, so rash.

Did they have no idea what he could do to them? Did Wasim really think that he could block Samson's way into Dareen's rooms? He could kill Samir, kill all of them if he so desired, and drag his bride away. The longing to do so grew stronger, but he forced himself to hold back.

Despite the familiar rage rising up within him, pulsing through every vein, he could not hurt Dareen's family. He glared at Wasim and spoke loudly enough for anyone standing behind the man in the house to hear. Let them know that they would cost the Philistines dearly for this act, this utterly unalterable act of betrayal.

"This time I cannot be blamed for everything I am going to do to you Philistines." With that, Samson turned on his heel and stalked off, but not before snatching up the goat and taking it with him.

Wheat harvest was nearly over for his family, though it was still going on in the rest of Israel. Samson's help had sped the process, so by the time he returned the goat to his father's pen, he knew he still had time to destroy the Philistines' crops, while his family's would be safe in the barns.

He stormed away from the house without even speaking to his mother or father and headed back to Philistine territory. He moved off the road to the fields where the wild animals roamed, climbed a low hill, and found a den of foxes. He stepped into the cave and counted the eyes staring out at him. Thirty foxes. Good. He found a large rock and rolled it over the cave's entrance, holding them captive.

He paced the hillside, searching for more foxes, finding more dens. He knew they liked this wild part of Philistine territory, and before long he had closed three hundred of them in their dens, unable to escape.

He stopped to scoop honey from a nearby hive, then sought thin vines to use as rope and short branches to act as torches. The pile grew in front of each cave, until he had one hundred fifty pieces, fit to tie the animals together, two at a time.

Satisfied with his work, he trudged toward a local town and snatched the larger torch standing near the gate when the guards' backs were turned. He half walked, half ran away from the city and headed back to the hills where the foxes could be heard crying to escape.

Their cries meant nothing to him in his quiet rage. Time to pay back the Philistines for what they had done to him. Hadn't God called him to destroy the enemy? Well, let them see what it was like to have their fields destroyed after all of the sheep and goats and grain they had taken from Israel over the years.

He set the torch in the ground, making sure it stood firm, rolled the first boulder away just enough to slip through, grabbed two foxes by the tails, and swiftly tied them together with a branch between their tails. He picked them up in one hand, shoved the rock over the cave again with his back, took the torch, and walked the pair toward a nearby Philistine grain field. He set the branch on fire and let them loose.

He turned about and headed back to the caves until he had repeated the task with all three hundred foxes, setting one hundred fifty Philistine fields on fire. Not one remained, not even their standing sheaves or uncut grain or olive groves or vineyards. In one late afternoon, they all burned to the ground.

Exhausted, Samson sank to the earth in one of the caves where the foxes had once slept. Tomorrow the Philistines would hear the full extent of the damage he had inflicted. And there would definitely be retribution, though Samson could not imagine how they could make things any worse for him.

CHAPTER TWELVE

Manoah hurried home from sitting at the city gate two days later and found Raya near the tree where the angel of the Lord had once appeared to her. "There is news," he said, catching his breath.

"Tell me." She stood, placed a hand on his shoulder, and beckoned him to sit, then offered him water from the skin she had brought with her. Fear slithered through her as she watched pain move across his face.

"Someone has set fire to the Philistines' fields, their standing grain, their olive groves, even their vineyards!" He gazed long at her, his suspicions betrayed in the knowing look he gave her.

"Samson," she whispered. "Samson did this."

"Who else would be so bold? Or angry? Or able? And the Philistines were told it was indeed our son." Manoah tossed his turban to the ground and ran both hands through his hair. "They will retaliate against us. Who knows what they will do? They could bring an entire army against our people or destroy our entire family." He searched her face. "I don't know what to do, Raya."

Her heart raced at his words, and she told herself to be calm. Growing as worried as he was would do them no good.

They must think. Plan. Pray. She glanced heavenward. "What if this was of the Lord?" She looked deeply into Manoah's eyes. "The angel told us that he would begin to destroy the Philistines before he was even born. What if this is part of the way God means to destroy them?"

"If God means to destroy them by taking their crops, all they have to do is steal ours. This seems more like Samson's revenge." Manoah stood and paced the small area, obviously unable to curb his anxious energy.

"How did you hear of this?" she asked, trying to turn his thoughts away from finding ways to blame their son.

"People coming for judgment from Samson brought the news. Though, of course, they did not find him at the gate. The Philistines are in an uproar and such news travels quickly, Raya." He stopped to face her. "The men who told the tale claim that Samson was seen setting fire to foxes and sending them into the fields, burning them to the ground."

Raya gasped. Foxes could be a menace to the lambs they raised but to set them ablaze? A shiver moved through her and she felt suddenly cold. This was not the son she had raised.

"There is more," Manoah said, at last coming to sit again, his energy apparently spent.

"Tell me." She knelt beside him.

"The Philistines believe Samson did this, whether they can prove it or not, so they took revenge on Samson's wife and father-in-law and burned them to death." Agony filled his features.

Raya placed a hand over her heart, again willing it to slow its rapid pacing. "Why take it out on them? They weren't the ones who burned the fields of their people."

"No, but according to those who came to the gate, Wasim gave Dareen to Samson's best man after Samson left the wedding and didn't return. That is why Samson destroyed the fields. So they took it out on Wasim and Dareen." Manoah's shoulders slumped and he leaned his back against a tree.

"I am having a hard time believing that our son did such a thing," Raya said. How could the son she raised do this? His temper had always been visible, but this rage...

"Believe it," Manoah said, interrupting her silent defense of her son.

"Samson will not let this rest. He will do more harm to the Philistines and it will simply escalate until they kill each other."

Raya placed her head in her hands. She knew this was his destiny, didn't she? From the start she knew he would be a Nazirite from birth to death and had no guarantee that he would live long. Especially if he continued to defy the Philistines like this.

Her heart ached with the thought of losing him, and yet a part of her had already done so, hadn't it? *Oh, Samson, my son. What have you done?* Would the Philistines retaliate against her and Manoah and burn them alive? A shudder caused her whole body to shake. Surely God would protect them.

But a moment later, as Manoah helped her to her feet, she met his gaze. "Should we leave Zorah? Take the family with us?" Though she had no idea where they could go.

"I will talk to Samson when he comes home. Hear the story from him and see what he plans to do next. If he thinks we should leave..." He paused and looked over the land. "If he thinks we would be safer to leave than to stay, we will go. But God help us if it comes to that."

Samson did not return home that evening or the next or even a week after the Philistines had killed his wife and father-in-law. People from outlying towns came to Zorah, seeking an audience with Samson to judge their cases, but he was nowhere to be found. Raya accompanied Manoah to the fields with the sheep, and together they searched some of the places Samson liked to go as a child. But there was no sign of him in the caves or fields or even nearby towns.

"I think we need to travel south," Manoah said one day after they had spent another week searching for him. "All of the reports tell us he was seen heading toward Judah. I will take my brothers with me. You must stay behind with the women and keep watch over the sheep." Dusk was settling over the town as they walked through its streets after another long day of searching.

Raya looked at him, seeing the weariness in the lines on his face, feeling that same weariness in her bones. They couldn't chase Samson to every place he chose to frequent. He'd been to many towns in Philistia and they had not known it. But she was not about to let Manoah travel to Judah or beyond without her. Samson was her son as much as his. If he went, she was going with him.

"You can't leave me home, Manoah. And I'm not sure it is wise to try to pursue him regardless. What can we do? We are no longer young, and this is a big undertaking. Even if you found him, would he listen to you? To me? He is determined to take vengeance on the Philistines, and I think we would just get in his way. Or worse, they would harm us and then he would be of no more use to the work of the Lord, for he would never get past losing us." She had paused as they neared their house, not wanting anyone in the family to hear their discussion.

"Our loss could make him angrier and his fight against the Philistines stronger." Manoah's reasoning troubled her, and she touched his arm, leaning in to look him in the eye.

"You can't mean that you would want harm to come to us to urge Samson to do more than he has already done." She waited, but he looked away, saying nothing. "If Samson has done this when it was only his father-in-law who perished—"

"Along with his bride." Manoah's interruption made her stop. They stood looking at each other.

"But we are his parents. He would not do well if harm came to us." She knew Samson too well. He would not be able to withstand worse treatment of his family than had already happened.

Manoah started walking again, and soon they entered the courtyard of their home. "Perhaps you are right. Going to Judah could prove fruitless, for Samson moves with the wind. By the time we arrived there, he could be back in Dan." He released a deep sigh. "I'm sorry, Raya. I cannot put you in harm's way, and yet I realize that I do not have the strength to stop this son, whom I do not understand. Perhaps you understand him better, for you carried him in the womb, but he has always been an enigma to me. His actions, his attitudes toward us—I have never understood him."

She took his hand as the moon's glow illuminated the courtyard. Voices came from inside the house, so she lowered hers so as not to be heard. "I do not understand him either, my husband. But he is our son. And he is God's chosen instrument for this time in history. All I can do for him is pray."

He nodded, defeat showing in his face. "I will do the same."

Samson rested his head on a handful of soft grasses he had picked from a nearby field and stretched his long body in a cave in the rock of Etam. Exhaustion washed over him, and his stomach rumbled from eating only berries and honey that he found along the path. Destroying the fields of so many Philistines in his fury over the loss of Dareen and Wasim brought some measure of comfort, but now he needed to fill his belly and sleep, and he couldn't decide which one he should do first. But food was nowhere to be found, so he opted for a chance to rest. He had dealt the Philistines a severe blow, and no doubt they would gather and come after him.

So he had run away and taken days to reach this cave near the town of Lehi in the land of Judah. Far from home. But he could not go home to his mother and father. The Philistines would simply find him and destroy his entire family.

No. It was safer here, though not the most comfortable of choices. He rolled onto his side and closed his eyes, but sleep eluded him. He shifted from side to side but at last could no longer ignore the rumbling in his stomach. There was no place to get bread at this hour. The town of Lehi would have already shut its gates.

He turned onto his stomach, but the stones ground through his tunic into his skin. Aggravated, he rose and left the cave, letting his eyes adjust to the moonlight. Lehi's lights shone in the distance, a short walk from these hills, though longer for lack of light to give him aid.

He moved slowly at first then picked up his pace as the stars grew brighter as though guiding his way. The gates of Lehi appeared, and he knocked on the side door, hoping a guard would give him entrance. He did not wish to destroy a town's protection in Israel just for want of bread.

The gate opened and a torch nearly blinded him, but the guard held it aside once he got a clear look at Samson.

"You are that Nazirite Samson," he said. "The one who is causing our enemy much trouble." The man smiled, as though he approved of Samson's actions.

"Yes," Samson replied, "but I am afraid my last efforts against them have left me without food or drink. Is there a place in town where I can still find a loaf of bread and a skin of water?" He could eat three times as much, but he did not wish to appear greedy.

The guard stepped aside and allowed Samson entrance. "We have more than that here at the guard station. Come. Follow me."

Samson looked about, tense, but when he saw no apparent enemy lurking, he followed at a distance. The guard entered a room, but Samson did not follow. He stood at the door and waited.

"Come in. You need not fear us. We are your brothers." The guard motioned him forward.

"And I am glad of it," Samson said. "But I prefer to take the bread and go." He leaned against the doorframe.

The guard tilted his head, regarding him, then gathered up cheese, bread, and a skin, and handed them to Samson. "Here, take them and go then, if you are more at ease doing so."

Samson looked at the food, his stomach gnawing, longing to take a bite, but one look at the skin and he handed it back. "This is wine, yes?"

"Yes. Our town's finest." The guard shifted his pointed staff from one hand to the other.

"I am a Nazirite. No wine has ever touched my lips. Might you have a skin of water instead?" He would have loved to accept the gift, for at that moment of weariness, his vow seemed pointless. But he waited, allowing the guard to take it from him and replace it with one of water. "Thank you."

"It is good to see that you are keeping your vow. It is not an easy thing to be called of God to do so." The guard met his gaze, and for a moment, Samson sensed he did not speak words of his own accord. As though God was speaking through him.

"No. It is not. But thank you." He turned and walked to the door, the guard following him.

"Be safe and well, Samson," the guard called after him.

Samson waved and nodded his thanks then disappeared quickly from the town's gate. Something about the place left him feeling odd, as though he was being watched. He took a different route back to the cave, ripping a large chunk of bread as he walked and stuffing it into his mouth. Tonight he would sleep and be strong again. Tomorrow he would see if he could find another way to stay fed and sheltered until he could escape the Philistines and discover another way to beat them at their cruel game of war.

CHAPTER THIRTEEN

Raya woke in a cold sweat, grateful it was just a dream. Or was it a dream? Samson! Something was happening to him or going to happen. She didn't know. The dream disappeared as a mist and she couldn't reach for it to pull it back into her thoughts no matter how hard she tried.

Manoah slept beside her, but her mind raced with concern. She must pray for her son. That had to be why she awakened. She crept from the bed, careful not to waken her husband, and knelt beside the cushions in the sitting area.

Oh, Adonai, You created my son, my Samson, to be Yours from the very beginning. He has kept Your vow, as far as I know, and he is beginning to rid Israel of the Philistine threat. But I fear that his life is in danger or that he is about to face the enemy in a new way that is going to tax his great strength. Please be with him, Lord. You are the Lord God Almighty who can save by many or by a few, and in this case You have only one. My only son. I do not know why You have not called others to his side to fight a war with our enemies, but for now, You have called him alone.

Guide him, Adonai. Walk beside him. Protect him. Give him the strength and insight he needs. Give him the wisdom to watch out for his own life, and send angels to watch over him. I would help him if only I could, but You have called me to do no more than pray. And yet

120

perhaps to pray for him is the best thing that I can do. May Your will be done.

She rose slowly, her feet tingling, and walked quietly about the room, looking through the window at the stars winking down at her. Peace settled as the words to her prayer reminded her that Samson was not alone. He belonged to God and God would answer. Surely God heard and was with Samson. Hadn't He been with him since before he was born? She breathed in and out and returned to her pallet at last, knowing that whether sleep came or not, she had done what she could. It was up to God to do the rest.

The next morning Samson awoke to the sound of warhorses and iron chariots crossing the fields not far from the cave where he lay hidden. He rose and peered into the early dawn and watched as the Philistines set up camp outside the gates of Lehi.

He had found help from the town for the past few days, but would their apparent friendliness aid him now that the Philistines were at their door ready to attack them?

He finished his dry bread from the night before and drank the water he'd left in the skin and waited, watching.

Dawn had barely risen above the trees when men poured out of the city of Lehi, marching directly toward the cave where he was staying. They had watched him leave their city and perhaps had him followed. He knew then that he could not trust them, as he had suspected from the beginning.

He did a quick count as he watched them climb the hill toward the cave. He could easily escape them and run hard toward home, but he sensed that waiting them out was the wiser choice. Perhaps God would use this to best the Philistines once again.

A large crowd of men from Judah approached the cave in the rock of Etam. As their feet came to a stop and a tentative silence followed, one of their leaders shouted to him. "Don't you realize the Philistines rule over us? What are you doing to us?"

Samson stepped from the spot where he was hidden to the mouth of the cave. "I only did to them what they did to me."

The leader looked him up and down. "We have come to tie you up and hand you over to the Philistines."

Samson hid a smile. No amount of rope could hold him as long as God was with him. As long as he did not break his vow and cut his hair or drink from the vine. "All right," he said. "But promise that you won't kill me yourselves."

The man nodded. "We will only tie you up and hand you over to the Philistines." The rest of the men closest to him murmured in agreement. "We won't kill you."

Samson stepped out of the cave and approached, his arms extended. Several men grabbed his arms, while two others tied new ropes around them. They led him down the incline and brought him to the Philistine encampment near Lehi.

The Philistines had turned to watch, and at the sight of Samson's approach shouted a victory cry. Laughter broke out among the camp, as Samson drew near and the men of Judah released him into their hands. The moment Samson was free of the men of Judah, they fled into Lehi and barred the door.

But Samson glanced heavenward and felt God's Spirit fill him with strength as He had done many times before. He snapped the ropes with one flick of his wrists and they fell to the ground.

He glanced about, as the Philistines seemed dumbstruck and suddenly afraid, despite their greater numbers. Samson looked at the ground and spotted the jawbone of a recently killed donkey. He grabbed it and began swinging it like a sword, moving this way and that, back and forth through the Philistine horde.

When the last Philistine lay dead or dying, he walked among the camp and counted the dead. One thousand men.

He gave a loud whoop and shouted toward the town of Lehi, to the frightened men who did not join him. "With the jawbone of a donkey, I've piled them in heaps! With the jawbone of a donkey, I've killed a thousand men!"

He walked away from the hill where the dead lay, watching as vultures circled overhead. He tossed the jawbone away and named the place Jawbone Hill.

He walked in the opposite direction of Lehi, no longer willing to take assistance from them, from men who could not be trusted. But a great thirst filled him, and he stumbled as he walked, looking for a well or a spring—someplace to draw water. Yet nothing appeared as he continued to walk, barely able to summon any more strength.

"Oh, Lord," he cried, "You have accomplished this great victory by the strength of your servant. Must I now die of thirst and fall into the hands of these pagans?" For he knew more Philistines would hear of his victory and soon chase him down again. And he could not trust his own people to keep from betraying him.

Was no one trustworthy in Israel? Even his God?

He closed his eyes and opened them again and suddenly he could see water gushing out of a hollow in the ground at Lehi, not far from the gates he had tried to get past. He scooped handful after handful into his mouth until he could hold no more.

He offered silent thanks to Adonai and called the place The Spring of the One Who Cried Out. Though people had failed him, perhaps God could be trusted after all.

CHAPTER FOURTEEN

Raya and Talia walked slowly to the town market near the eastern gate of the city. More than three months had passed with no word from Samson. Not even a rumor as to his whereabouts, though men from other cities still came to seek him out. How could he ignore his duties to act as judge as he had been doing for so long?

And how could he stay away from his parents without a word? She glanced at Talia, who swung a basket in her left hand. At her look, Talia met her gaze.

"You are quiet today," Talia said, her brows knit in concern. "You are worried about Samson." It wasn't a question, and Raya simply nodded her response.

"But didn't you know that God would lead him away to fight the Philistines? He can't do that from Zorah, Raya. Though I do think he should have sent some word."

Raya looked away, wiping a tear that slipped from her eye. "We don't even know if he is alive or dead." She blinked hard, forcing back the emotion that always lived on the surface of late. What had happened to her song? Her peace? She had been unable to find either of them for far too long.

Talia stopped, touched Raya's arm, and glanced around them. The market booths were still some distance away and they were alone on the path at the moment. "What do you feel here?" She touched her middle, where her people believed the seat of the emotions was centered. "What does it tell you? Would not a mother know if her son were living or dead?"

Raya touched her middle as well and pondered Talia's words. "He lives. I do not know where, but he lives." Relief filled her as she felt sudden confirmation in her heart. Was this Adonai's way of comforting her? But why then did Samson remain so silent?

"What if I sent Amichai and Chaim to a few nearby cities to check? Ask around to see if anyone has heard from him?" Talia smiled and began walking again toward the market.

Raya fell into step with her. "That would ease my mind. To know he is safe. Or to even know where he is…though I would not ask that they enter the cities of the Philistines. I would not ask your sons to take that risk."

Talia regarded her. "They are grown, strong men. Let us see what they choose to do. But I will warn them to be on their guard. Perhaps they will find a shepherd in the hills who knows something. Or a wanderer from other lands."

"Anything would be helpful." Raya breathed easier as she approached the cheese maker and chose a round of cheese. Gratitude filled her, though at the same time she sent a silent prayer heavenward. If God did not go with the young men, they would not be successful. And the one thing she did not know was whether God wanted her son to be found.

True to her word, Talia and Elead sent their sons in search of Samson. Raya walked in the fields with Manoah, watching the sheep as they anxiously awaited word. Raya slipped her arm through her husband's and squeezed, leaning closer. "I hope they find out something."

Manoah nodded, though when he spoke his voice rasped. "As do I." He cleared his throat then coughed slightly. "And I hope it is soon."

Raya watched him, certain the cough and strange sound in his throat were from a simple illness, as they contracted them from time to time. But as she continued to look at him out of the corner of her eye, she saw his gait slacken, slower than he used to be, and he used his staff as though he needed it to hold him up. Was Manoah's health failing?

He was older than she was by several years, and they were not young when Samson was born. He'd worked hard in the fields all of his life. Was age starting to wear him down?

Her heartbeat quickened as a sudden fear of losing him coursed through her. She nearly stumbled along the grassy ground. The sheep grazed in the nearby pasture as the two of them inspected each one as they passed by. But the distraction of the sheep, the watching for predators, and her constant worry about Samson were not enough to stop this fear for Manoah. *Please, Adonai, I cannot lose him.* Should she mention her fears to her husband? Was Manoah feeling well or did he struggle in silence?

They sat on the grass and she pulled food from the basket she carried, offering him some. He took a few bites but then pushed the rest away. "Save it for later," he said. "I'm not quite hungry yet."

She met his gaze, showing him her concern. "Manoah, tell me honestly, are you unwell?"

He lifted his brows. "Unwell? Why would you ask such a thing? Because I'm not hungry at the moment?" Irritation laced his words.

"You were coughing and you seem tired. I am simply concerned," she said, knowing that his defensiveness meant more than he was saying.

"I'm fine, Raya. Samson wears me down, if you want the truth. Your worry over him wears me down. We cannot guide him any longer. He is a man grown. He is stubborn and apparently God is leading him to places we cannot go. So yes, I'm weary. Weary of him for not contacting us and weary of your worries over him."

She leaned back as though struck. "I am sorry to have upset you then. A mother tends to worry, and how can I help it when he will not contact us? What is a mother to do?"

"Trust that Adonai watches over him now as He did before he was born. Surely we can do that, can't we?" Manoah coughed again, and she realized that weariness over Samson or her worries was not all that troubled him. His response was to keep her from also worrying over him. But his response was not working.

"I can trust Adonai, my husband. But I would like you to tell me when this weariness becomes more than your own concerns for our son or for me. If you are ill, I can find some herbs. Do not keep me from helping you. I cannot lose you." She heard her voice rise on the last words. She clamped her mouth shut, unwilling to allow emotion to rule her again.

"You will not lose me," he said, taking her hand. "I am afraid you are stuck with me for many years to come." He smiled, but it did not reach his eyes. And she found no mirth in his words.

"I'd better," she said, smiling to cover what he would not say. For this once she did not believe him, and she knew she was at God's mercy to keep her from losing both husband and son.

A week later, Talia's sons returned as dusk was settling over the town. They entered the courtyard and found their father already seated with the other men eating the evening meal.

"You are back," Elead said, stating what everyone saw to be true as though he could think of nothing else to say.

"Did you find him?" Raya blurted the words as she approached her nephews.

Anxious looks passed between them, and she felt the ominous kick of dread fill her.

"We found someone who told us about him," Chaim said. "But I would rather tell Uncle Manoah first. Aunt Raya, I fear you will not like what you hear."

Raya straightened her spine and faced her nephews. "Whatever you have to say to my husband, I would hear as well. Please speak." She did not even glance at Manoah to see whether he approved of her insistence that she stay to listen. This was her son! She would not have the entire household knowing the truth while she waited in the dark.

"We found an Israelite leaving the city of Gath. He'd gone there to have his tools sharpened, and we stopped to talk with him," Amichai said.

"When we asked after Samson, he had one wild tale to tell," Chaim interjected.

Raya watched both boys' eyes widen as though they still were not sure if they believed it themselves. She tapped an impatient foot.

"They said Samson had been to Gaza to visit a prostitute." The words hung in the air, and Raya sucked in a breath attempting to regain her bearings. A prostitute? A Nazirite would not break one of the basic moral laws of God. But apparently he did.

"You are sure of this?" Manoah asked.

"As sure as the man could be. The Philistines heard he was there, so they waited at the town gates to ambush him at the light of dawn. Apparently they planned to kill him." Amichai drew a hand along his beard.

"But somehow Samson heard of it and left the prostitute at midnight," Chaim said. The young men shared a glance. "Samson rose from the bed, went to the city gates, grabbed hold of the doors to the town gate, including the two posts that hold the doors along with the bars that keep them closed, and lifted them in his hands! They say he carried them on his shoulders all the way to the top of a hill across from Hebron. That's nearly forty miles!"

Raya sank onto a cushion, her legs no longer willing to hold her up. "Did they pursue him?" she asked at last.

"I don't think so. I don't think they knew what to do or how he got away from them. Most of them had probably fallen asleep, thinking Samson would stay in the city until dawn," Amichai said.

"He is safe then." Manoah's voice was barely above a whisper. Raya looked at him sharply but saw only an expression of relief in his eyes.

Tension slowly left Raya's body. Manoah was right. Samson was safe. For now. But oh, Adonai, why did he think he needed to visit a Philistine prostitute? *How could you?* But her son was not there to ask, and what could she say to him even if he suddenly appeared?

Did her son honestly think that as long as he didn't cut his hair and didn't drink from the vine or touch a dead thing that he was doing all God required? He knew the law! Manoah had taught it to him. Samson had judged cases using the very laws he was now breaking by committing fornication.

Raya glanced at Talia and could not hide the sorrow that suddenly filled her. Tears threatened, and she pushed up from the cushion and fled the room. Let the other women feed the men and eat together. She was no longer hungry.

CHAPTER FIFTEEN

Raya arose the next morning, head pounding and sick to her stomach. She rolled onto her side and forced weary legs to stand. When did every muscle decide to ache? Had she contracted the same malady that seemed to be troubling Manoah?

One glance at the window told her the sun had already risen and she was late helping to prepare the morning meal. Manoah was nowhere to be seen, which meant he had likely already taken the sheep to the fields.

Why had she not wakened before him and fulfilled her morning duties, as a good wife should? The memories of Amichai and Chaim's report of Samson hit her like a fist to her middle. She stumbled and caught herself, leaning heavily against the wall. *Samson. Oh my son!*

Sudden weakness filled her and she made her way to the couch and sank onto the cushions, not caring that the sound of the millstone and female chatter could be heard in the courtyard nearby. She had never expected to bear a son. Though she had prayed for one, she had not believed it possible after years upon years of barrenness. And then the angel appeared. All of her former sadness had disappeared as she bore and raised her beloved son to follow Adonai's ways. Where had she gone wrong? She had done all she knew to train him the way the law prescribed, and yet nothing she had taught him seemed to have mattered. Had he cut his hair as well?

Her heart ached with pain so raw she wondered if she would see blood seeping through her chest. She looked, but her tunic was dry. Her eyes, on the other hand, were not, for she could not stop the tears. Silent sobs grew from a place deep within her and she curled onto her side, weeping into the cushions. Surely she had failed him. If she had been a better mother. If she had watched him more closely, taught him more passionately, given him more freedoms of those he could have, maybe then he would not have strayed so far from the word of the Lord.

Oh, Adonai, forgive me. You gave me one son and one task—to raise him—and I failed You. I longed to pass on to him the same love I have for You, but he did not find it. He cannot see You the way I do. Why was Your law given to him but Your presence kept from him? Was it kept from him? Or did he push You away?

Tormenting thoughts and memories of a little boy who wrapped his arms around her neck and nodded in wide-eyed wonder when she told him of his birth and the angel's visit mocked her now. What good had it ever done to pray over him as he slept? Where were the answers to the longings of her heart? Why give her such a gift and blessing of a child, only to have him become her source of constant heartache and sorrow?

Must I have sorrow in my heart every day?

But even as she lifted her head, hoping for an answer, she heard nothing. No whisper of hope or promise of future joy. No feeling of commendation rather than the condemnation she heaped upon herself. Samson was supposed to begin to deliver Israel from the hand of the Philistines. He was supposed to have obeyed the vow of the Nazirite all of his life. He was supposed to bring them and their nation great joy.

At least she had hoped and expected that he would bring their nation joy. She had always hoped he would fulfill all that God had for him. All that God wanted him to be. Why did it seem like he had pushed it all away?

A soft knock on her door roused her, and she sat up, wiping her eyes with both hands. She was in no shape to speak to anyone, especially a member of her family. She needed to escape, not face them. For though they might not say so, she often sensed judgment behind their smiles.

Even if Talia stood on the other side of that door, she could not face her. She rose as quietly as she could, snatched her robe, and slipped out the side door, even as she heard Talia call her name.

She closed the door behind her and ran toward the woods. Solitude and space to think—that was what she needed now. Surely she could pull herself together given enough time. Or perhaps she should run after Samson, search every Philistine city until she found him, and drag him home. It was a desire that often surfaced.

But she knew she could never follow through with it. She would fall along the path or be attacked by wild animals. She had not practiced with a sling enough to defend herself. She had never traveled far from home and had no courage to do so now.

She reached the edge of the woods and moved into the clearing where she always came for sanctuary. Where she had met the angel of the Lord. But as her eyes adjusted to the dimness, she looked down and found Manoah facedown in the dirt. She stood frozen, her scream echoing in the trees around her.

"Manoah?" She found her strength and rushed to his side, then felt his neck and turned him as best she could, listening for breath. "Manoah, please! Can you hear me?"

He did not answer, but when she leaned against his mouth, she felt his slight breath. She rolled him over and checked him for injuries. Finding none, she turned and raced back to the house for help. What had caused him to come to her sanctuary and why could he not speak to her?

Oh, Adonai! Help me!

Reaching the house, she burst through the front door. "Talia! Karmela! Help me!"

When Elead and Ariel appeared before their wives did, she breathed in relief. They had not yet gone to the fields.

"You must come at once. Manoah lies in the woods, and I cannot rouse him."

They did not bother to grab a cloak or walking stick but ran ahead of her in the direction she told them. She followed as fast as she could, panting and praying, forgetting her former fears and angst over her son. Her husband mattered to her more now. She could not lose him. But as the men carried him back to the house, she had little hope that anything could save him.

Samson tossed the gates of Gaza in a field outside of Hebron. The relief from the loss of their weight surprised him. He hadn't seemed to notice the burden during his long walk out of Philistine lands. He'd stopped several times to check over his shoulder to see if anyone followed, but even with the light of dawn, no one traveled behind him.

He glanced heavenward at the sun now making its way to the midpoint in the sky. His stomach rumbled with that fierce hunger he often got when he did something that used his strength. He walked along the field toward a copse of trees. Where vegetation grew, water must be near. To slake his thirst and find food—he could think of nothing more.

He half ran, half walked the distance to the trees, watching their leaves sway in the breeze. Stopping, he listened for the sound of water. Could this simply be a forest without a nearby spring? He heard nothing and walked on, frustration building. Would God let him die of hunger and thirst because he'd slept with Daslima, a prostitute? He slowed his step, a twinge of guilt filling him. Women were his weakness. Philistine women. He knew this. Had known it since he'd first laid eyes on Dareen. Had known it in every Philistine town he had explored.

Was such a desire so bad? He had hurt his parents by not choosing a Hebrew wife. He knew that too. But none in his tribe appealed to him. A strong man needed a strong woman, a beautiful woman. And no one near his age had ever met his standards for a wife. But he could not make his father see that. He did not even try to explain his need to Imma. She had been too hurt by his marriage to Dareen. Better for her that she never learned of Daslima. Or any other Philistine woman he might choose.

He fisted his hands as he walked on, stopping to listen now and then to more than the crunch of twigs and stones beneath his feet. At last the soft gurgle of a stream filled his ears, and he hurried his step. He knelt at the stream's edge and scooped handfuls of water into his mouth.

Satisfied, though still hungry, he sat near the bank and took in his surroundings. He was far from Philistine territory, probably past Hebron by now. He should find a city and purchase bread, but if he could catch a gazelle, he could have food for days. The trick would be to find where the pack grazed and outrun one, for he had no bow or sling to shoot at them.

He took another drink and stood, assessing his position, then set off to hunt some type of meat. Bread might satisfy, but he wanted more. Even if he had to kill a coney or a hare, though they were unclean animals, he would do it. He ignored the guilt that came with that thought. He had broken so many of God's laws already, he wasn't sure he would ever be forgiven. What did it matter if he broke one more?

Raya placed a cool cloth over Manoah's forehead while Talia spooned herbal broth into his mouth, wiping the spills that slipped through his partly opened lips. The men and Raya herself had searched his body from head to foot and found the puncture wounds of a snake on one ankle. The women had frantically made poultices to draw out the poison, while the men had gone in search of the reptile to kill it.

"Please, Manoah, my husband, won't you wake up?" Raya knelt at his side and laid her head on his chest, grateful for its rise and fall. He had improved a little since she had found him, but he had yet to open his eyes and speak to her.

"He will get well, Raya," Talia said, coming up beside her and resting her hand on Raya's shoulder. "Now that we know what caused it, Karmela is making another poultice. We will not stop until all of the poison is gone."

"If that is all that it is. What of his cough and weariness before this happened?" She hated the fear that dogged her steps and the blame she felt every time she realized that her constant worry and complaints over Samson might have worn him down, made him succumb to such a thing as this.

"It's not your fault, Raya. Manoah was as burdened by Samson as you are. He told Elead as much. His cough was a simple illness. If you recall, he had begun to improve before he was bitten." Talia turned as Karmela approached with a new poultice.

Karmela bent over Manoah's leg, removed the old poultice, felt along his ankle, and replaced the old poultice with the new one. "There is less fire in his leg," she said, looking at Raya. "He will get well. You will see." She left them then, not one to talk much, and returned to the cooking area to begin meal preparations.

"We should help her," Raya said, though she did not move from Manoah's side.

"The girls will help her. And I will join them. You will stay here." She knelt at Raya's side. "Raya, look at me."

Raya obeyed, reading kindness in her eyes. "I know you fear for Manoah as you also fear for Samson. Both of you do and it has taken a toll on you. Samson's life has changed our entire family. His very birth was a miracle of God." She cupped Raya's shoulder. "You did everything God asked of you to teach him the ways of our God. But Samson is still a man of his own. Each one of us must decide whether to obey the laws we are taught or not. Each one of us must decide whether our God will become our God in a real way. We can be like those in this family who obey without much thought—without prayer or longing for God. Or we can yearn to know Him as you and Manoah do." She pushed the hair from Raya's eyes, and Raya blinked back tears.

"But know this," she continued, "just because Samson knows the truth does not mean he wants to obey it. Just because God called him to be a Nazirite does not mean he wanted to embrace his calling. He still has to choose. And even if he is disobeying his vows now, our God can still call him back to Himself. Think of our ancestors Judah and his brothers and what they did to Joseph. Eventually, many years later, God brought them together again and Joseph forgave them. If Joseph, a mere man, can forgive, our God can forgive Samson and restore all of these years he is wasting."

Raya released a deep sigh at Talia's words. Hope-filled words. She hugged Talia and leaned back on her heels. "Thank you. I know you are right. I do not know if I will live to see Samson return to keep his vow, but I know that if he still lives, God is still at work in him. I have always known his life would be hard. I just did not realize that his calling would also be hard on both of us. And I am especially concerned about what his actions are doing to Manoah." She glanced at her sleeping husband and sighed.

"You feel this way because you both want to make him into what God wants, but only God can make us into the person He desires us to be." Talia stood then. "I will see if I am needed and return to sit with you. In the meantime, do not fear. Manoah will get well, and Samson will come home again. Just wait and see."

Raya nodded as Talia left the room. Talia always saw the good in everything, the hope in the future. She should have been Samson's mother, for then perhaps Samson would have not been so restless as he grew with his vow. But God had chosen her for the blessing and the trial this son had caused her. Despite everything, she was glad of it.

PART FOUR

Some time later Samson fell in love with a woman named Delilah, who lived in the valley of Sorek. The rulers of the Philistines went to her and said, "Entice Samson to tell you what makes him so strong and how he can be overpowered and tied up securely. Then each of us will give you 1,100 pieces of silver."

    —Judges 16:4–5 (NLT)

CHAPTER SIXTEEN

Months passed and Manoah improved day by day until Raya could at last breathe easier. Though he walked with a slight limp now, he no longer carried the burden of weariness or pain she had seen in him during his recovery.

Word had come to them from men seeking Samson's counsel that their son had been seen in the Valley of Sorek, Philistine territory. He had taken residence with a woman there. Not a prostitute but not his wife. Delilah. The name did not sit well on Raya's tongue.

She worked with Karmela and Talia in the family courtyard one summer morning, grinding the wheat kernels in silence, her mind moving between thoughts of Samson and the conversation going on around her.

"Without Samson home this year for grape harvest, Chaim said we could celebrate not only at the wine pressing but here afterward as the rest of our clan does in their homes. There is no need not to drink the wine with our meals and feel the joy it brings." Shayna's words caught Raya's ears, and she stopped the grindstone.

"Shayna!" Talia said, giving her daughter-in-law a pointed look.

"What? Surely Raya knows how we have sacrificed drinking wine in this house to keep Samson from breaking his vow. But it sounds like he cares nothing for the laws of God or his Nazirite promises. Since he is not here, why should we be forced to please him?" Shayna's tone held more than a little contempt, and Raya felt as though she had suffered a blow. Was this how her family had felt about her son all these years?

"We pleased Manoah and Raya so they could help Samson keep his vow," Talia said, crossing her arms over her chest. "We did so willingly from the time Samson was born. I will not tolerate such disrespect now to Raya and Manoah simply because you want to bring wine into this house!"

Tension fell like a pall over the women. The younger daughters-in-law looked at one another, their expressions revealing displeasure. Karmela continued to knead the dough and did not look up or even seemed to have heard the confrontation.

Raya sat back, her heart pounding, not knowing how to respond or what to do. She tried to pray, but no words would come to her heart. At last, when the silence grew too strong, she lifted her head and looked from one woman to the other. Only Karmela avoided her gaze.

"Shayna does have a point," Raya said, forcing her words to carry kindness instead of the hurt the girl's attitude had brought. "Samson was the one who was commanded by the vow not to drink of the fruit of the vine, nor to even taste a raisin or grape. Though I do thank you that you did try to make it easier for him. He was...is...easily tempted." She stopped, unable to say more, and turned away from their scrutiny. The grindstone weighted her hand, and she turned it once more, letting the noise replace whatever response they gave.

She wanted to flee. Why did she always want to run from conflict? And what did that say about her trust in Adonai if she could not even face people who distressed her with their words? She must be stronger than this! Surely they had a right to express their views. And she was not so weak that she could not accept their differences. It had been her decision to stay behind from these feasts with her son. She had asked the family to make it easier on Samson. But Samson was no longer living here. Their desires were perfectly understandable.

She drew a deep breath and briefly closed her eyes, willing herself to find good, even pleasure in the work, focusing on the feel of the stone pressing against each kernel, breaking the outer layer in order to turn the seed into something they could make into bread.

Soft conversation about going to market and weaving the next set of clothes for the grandchildren of Karmela and Talia turned the tone lighter, but Raya still focused on the wheat kernels breaking apart, their shells opening up to the hidden, life-giving food beneath. How often had she performed this task? And yet she had never once pondered the work or how like life a kernel of wheat could be.

Is this what You do to teach us, Adonai? Are these trials we face like the grinding of wheat, stripping our outer protection to reveal something useful within? Was that what God was doing with her? Breaking her heart to make her something new?

The thought brought the sting of emotion and she abruptly stopped her work. She sifted the flour in her hand then pulled the bowl from the millstone and poured the soft flour into the sieve to sift the remaining hard shells from the finer flour. Grinding. Breaking. Sifting. Her mind turned with too many thoughts.

"Raya, are you all right?" Talia asked, as she stopped her own sifting of the stones from the lentils.

Raya looked up and met Talia's gaze. "I don't know. I think so. But it is not something I can explain." Nor would she. Not here. Not now. She would finish the work and then walk for a time in the fields, where she could ponder the symbolism her mind had just seen.

How long had she been like the dry kernels under God's millstone? Was Samson undergoing the same thing? Did God take each person and mold him or her, as Talia had once said, by breaking their self-protection to reveal the person He had always intended they should be?

Oh but how hard it was to learn such things! If losing Samson was God's way of teaching her, she was not sure she wanted it. How could she? To lose the son, the gift, to sacrifice all—why would God even ask it of her?

Did Samson feel the same loss when he thought of her or Manoah? Or did they not even come to his mind? Would God care enough to teach Samson to sacrifice all? Was that not part of his Nazirite calling?

A deep sigh lifted her chest and she struggled to release it. She could not imagine a worse pain than Samson's actions had brought to her heart. And Samson was not a father. He could not understand how a child could wound a parent. He could not be changed in that way.

So what will You use to teach him? Her silent prayer lifted heavenward as she stood and handed Karmela the last of the wheat. What would it take to help Samson see that breaking the laws of God was not something a man of God should do?

Samson opened the door to Delilah's house and pulled it closed behind him. He did not bother to knock or ask her permission to enter any longer as he had done during the first few weeks of their whirlwind encounter. She had won him with a look where he found her near the spring in Sorek's valley. The veil revealing those captivating eyes had drawn him with her irresistible charm.

"Are you home?" he called, as he looked over the sprawling house. Delilah's was one of the few houses dotting the valley, set above the waters that moved through the basin. How she managed to live here was still a mystery to him. Somehow she found a way to sell her wares, even without a husband to help support her.

Why Delilah had remained alone these many years also puzzled him. Her beauty could have moved many a man to want her, yet she did not sell her body to any of them. Marriage would have given her children to raise and a man to care for. But she seemed content in this wilderness with only a handful of distant neighbors.

He rubbed a hand along his braided beard as he walked to the sleeping chamber. "Delilah?" Perhaps, if he used enough persuasion, he could be the man who changed her mind about a husband and children.

He paced the length of the house, checked the courtyard and the garden behind the house. Still no sign of her. Had she wandered off with those few goats of hers?

He thought to leave and look for her, but instead he sank onto her cushioned couch and watched the door. She would come. And if she didn't, he would look for her at dawn.

A yawn overtook him, and he rested his head against the soft pillow. Delilah usually ran her fingers through the unbraided part of his hair near his temples and coaxed him to sleep after a good meal and a rousing night of passion.

He sat up, irritated that she was not waiting for him, and more so that he found himself so concerned for her welfare. She had proven that she could take care of herself, so why was he suddenly worried for her safety? Where could she be?

She didn't need him to look after her. And yet he pushed to his feet regardless and strode to the door. He stood outside, searching the area in the deepening dusk for some sign of her, then walked the length of the land near her house all the way to one of her neighbors.

As he neared the closest home tucked away in the hills, she emerged from the dwelling carrying a torch. Light came from inside the house, a dwelling smaller than Delilah's but one that housed a Philistine family. He glimpsed several men standing in the doorway as she parted. She glanced back at them and smiled, then turned toward her house.

Who were those men? What did Delilah want with them? They were not all of the same family, were they? A thousand questions filled his mind as he ducked into the shadows, stepping away from the hillside closer to the valley floor.

He glanced back at the house where he had seen the men, but the door was shut now, the light flickering behind high windows. He would find out nothing unless he waited for them to leave. But then what was he to do? Approach them? Demand why they had met with Delilah?

Anger tingled the back of his neck and flowed through his veins. The desire to enter the house and tear those men limb from limb surged through him. But as the sun fully set and night owls hooted and bats sailed in the air above him, he tamped his anger and drew in a calming breath. If he destroyed Delilah's neighbors now, she would reject him, and worse, he would not find a way to defeat a larger number of Philistines that he might meet with her help.

No. Better to wait for another day. He would not even ask her what she had been doing. Could he stop himself from coaxing her to divulge her secrets? But he must.

He warred with himself as he climbed the hill and walked in silence toward her house, many paces behind her now. She opened the door and left the torch burning in a niche in the ground, a light to protect her from the overwhelming darkness. The one weakness in her otherwise amazing inner strength was a secret she had revealed to him during their first days together—she feared the darkness.

He took comfort that she seemed to calm in the reassurance he had given her, promising to protect her from anyone and anything that might come against her. He had feared she would rebuff him and tell him that she did not need a man, but instead she had repaid him with more passion than even the prostitute had given to him. A smile skirted his lips. Would a Hebrew wife have been as giving of herself or as confident of his abilities?

He pushed the thought aside as he reached her courtyard and opened the door. "Delilah. I came earlier and you were not here. I expected to find you at home." He sank onto the couch and looked at her where she stood setting bread onto a board then cutting into a large cheese to set before them.

"Ah, my darling. You missed me?" Her voice held a cultured tone. "I stopped to see if Ethar needed anything. You know her son has not felt well these past few days." She came closer and touched his cheek, her smile seductive.

Samson searched her face, assessing her with a look. She was lying and they both knew it. But he did not say so. He could tell by the way her mouth tightened ever so slightly at the corners. And the fact that he had seen the men she had spoken to. If the boy was so sick, why were the men visiting?

He grasped her hand and kissed her fingers. "Of course. You had to do what you could. But you will be the death of me, woman. I worried when I did not find you. You must tell me when you plan to be so long."

She laughed, delighting him. "I cannot be bound to your rules, my love. But come now. We are here and both hungry. Let us eat and then make up for the time we have lost." She squeezed his fingers, and he returned it.

"My, but you are strong!" She pulled her hand from his, laughing. "How is it possible that a mere man can carry such strength?" She turned to him then and ran her hand over his chest. "Surely there is some secret you are keeping from me. No human has ever been so strong as to carry the weight of Gaza's city gate all the way to Hebron!"

He cupped her cheek, then reached around her and snatched a piece of the cheese she had cut. "It is a gift from my God," he said, gently setting her aside. "I cannot argue with God when He chooses to give me a gift, now can I?"

She curled her lower lip in a pout. "You toy with me, Samson. No god can give a man such strength. If he could, every Philistine in the land would pay great sums for such a treasure! Surely there is another reason." She clung to his arm even as he plopped another piece of cheese into his mouth, trying to avoid her probing question.

"Please, Samson, tell me what makes you so strong and what it would take to tie you up securely." He looked at her, unnerved that she should ask him such a thing. Never in the months he had spent with her had she acted as though she wanted to see him bound and caught. Had those men put her up to this? Was that the real reason she had gone to visit Ethar?

"Why should you ask me such a thing? Are you trying to get rid of me, my love?" The thought wounded, as though his love for her meant nothing to her at all.

She glanced beyond him then faced him again, her smile bright. "I am simply curious. You must know that every Philistine in the land wonders how you are able to do so much. You have to admit, you have done us harm, Samson. To know the source of your strength is something anyone would ask." She curled her fingers around his forearm and pulled him toward the couch. "But never mind that tonight. One day you will trust my love enough to tell me."

Samson followed her like a helpless lamb, his pulse quickening with every step. She was a frustrating woman. But she would make every moment of this night one of pleasures he could not resist. She had a way of coaxing him to want to tell her everything. Even the answer to this blatant question. Those men had put her up to asking him, he was sure of it. The Philistines had wanted to capture him for years. But he could not give in to her, not even to appease her.

Thankfully, she let the matter rest for now. Perhaps she would stop asking and go on with the life they had begun. Was that too much to ask?

No matter how seductive she became, he could not give in to her. His manhood he could give her. His heart she had already stolen. But his secret must remain his alone.

CHAPTER SEVENTEEN

Five Years Later

Raya stood at the fork in the road where Manoah and Elead had gone toward the Valley of Sorek three days before, once again searching for information of Samson. She pulled the cloak tightly about her, warding off the chill of the fall breeze. The deeper cold that caused her to tremble did not come from the air about her, though she closed herself in just the same. This inner chill ran through her, to her very bones.

Did Samson still live? He had been gone so long. She closed her eyes, trying to see his face in her mind's eye. Every year it grew dimmer, and the feel of his arms around her was a distant memory. She blinked, hating the emotion that dogged her steps. How was it possible that she still ached for him when he had obviously abandoned them? Word had come that he still judged Israel, but he had moved to a different city and judged them closer to Philistine territory.

Why would he do that? Still he remained with that woman Delilah. A woman not his wife. And in all of his time away from them, there had been no word of any more Philistines dying in battle against him as had happened in his younger years.

Why won't you come home? She placed a hand over her heart, sure it would stop beating at any moment, but it kept on and on, her life one of constant struggle just to keep believing, keep trusting that God was with her and with her son. Why else would He have made Samson if not for good? Why then did her life since his coming into adulthood feel so terribly bad?

She opened her eyes, shading them against the early-morning glare, willing them to see her husband returning with news. But as the sun rose in the sky, there was no sign of Manoah or Elead. Her husband's insistence on going instead of sending their nephews was just a sign of his stubbornness. The man still walked with a limp. Did he think he could defend himself against a predator? Two old men thinking they could find information better left to others, to those younger?

She pulled the scarf over her head and turned back toward the house. To wait was so hard. Her life had been one of constant waiting. She kicked a stone on the path and watched her feet, aged now, walk with a slowness that came from sorrow. She really needed to get past this longing for a son who was obviously not coming home. Despite her prayers, her silent tears, her aching heart, God was not answering. And she could not make Him do so.

She reached the courtyard, where Karmela bustled about setting food out to be prepared for the evening meal. This sister-in-law whose children remained in their home and followed the Law of Moses without question, glanced at her, then stopped her work.

"No word?" Karmela rarely asked after Samson or seemed to care that Raya suffered. It had been the bane of Raya's life to live with a woman who expected nothing from God, rarely talked about Him or even prayed. Yet her life was everything Raya wished hers could be.

Raya shook her head, heat filling her face at the jealousy rising within her. Karmela's trust or lack of trust in God was not Raya's business. Maybe she prayed silently or kept the law so well that God blessed her even during those times when she seemed indifferent to the things of the Lord. Karmela was hard to understand, but Raya still struggled with wanting to understand her.

"Perhaps they will return later," Karmela said softly.

Raya met her gaze, surprised at her show of concern. "Perhaps." Though she knew they could be gone yet for days. What if something happened to them along the way? Was it too soon to send her nephews to look for them? "I never should have told them I longed for news of him." She looked away and turned toward the door of the house.

"You did nothing any mother wouldn't have done. We have all wondered why Samson stays away. His behavior is not normal for a son of Israel." Karmela stepped closer, touched Raya's arm. "I have never told you, but I am sorry you suffer so because of him. Your life has not been as easy as mine has been. I have found it hard to share your concerns or feelings like Talia can." She stepped back at Raya's surprised look. "But I wanted you to know that I pray for him too." She turned then, leaving Raya stunned. And doubly confused.

"Thank you," she said to Karmela's retreating back as the woman returned to her tasks. Raya opened the door and hurried to her rooms, her heart pounding with even more questions than she had carried with her to watch the road.

Why, Adonai? Karmela prays for my Samson. She does everything right and her children follow You. Yet You chose my son to be a Nazirite, set apart for his life to You. Why is Your choice so painful for the mother of such a child? It would have been easier to remain barren.

She didn't mean that. She couldn't mean that. Samson had been the joy of her life for every year that he had lived with them. She would not take back the memories of his kiss on her cheek or his chubby hand in hers as they walked along the way and talked about his vow. She wouldn't give him back even if she could. She loved him! Perhaps she loved him too intensely.

Did he feel that she wanted to know too much, be too close to him, while he longed to flee to the women of the Philistines? Was his disobedience to the vow, to the Law of Moses so great that he was ashamed to come home and face them again?

If only she could tell him that it didn't matter. Whatever he had done, she would not judge him or hold it against him. And if he but asked, God would surely accept a sacrifice and forgive him.

She buried her head in the cushions, too weary to even pray. Would that there was a way for her to find him, to tell him all was forgiven, just come home! Would that Manoah and Elead could find him and convince him to return.

But she dared not ask it of Adonai. She had asked every day, at least three times a day, and God had remained silent.

Perhaps He would hear Karmela's prayers since He seemed to give her everything pleasant in life. Perhaps she should stop caring and let others carry this burden that was tearing her apart.

Perhaps... If only she could. But how did a mother forget the son of her womb? How did a mother stop praying for a lost sheep to be found? She only knew that she could not. Even though every part of her longed to be free of this burden and have reason to rejoice and sing again.

Another week passed before Manoah and Elead finally returned home. Raya ran to her husband as he leaned on his walking stick, Elead at his side. She clung to him a moment, then searched his face. "Tell me what you know," she said.

Manoah stopped and looked at his brother. "Go on ahead to your family. We will come along soon. And thank you for joining me on this trip."

Elead nodded. "What else are brothers for?" He glanced at Raya then moved down the path toward home. When he was out of earshot, Raya looked into Manoah's eyes again.

"Tell me," she repeated. "What did you learn?"

Manoah stroked his beard then took her hand and coaxed her to walk with him to a large stone near the side of the road where they could sit. She sat as he directed and he beside her.

"Samson still resides with Delilah in the Valley of Sorek. He judges Israel in Beth-Shemesh and returns to her home at night."

"Did you see him?" Raya's heart picked up its pace, and she suddenly wished she had gone with him.

Manoah nodded. "We saw him. In Beth-Shemesh. We spoke to him after he finished judging for the day."

Raya felt suddenly weak and grateful she was sitting, for she knew her legs would not have held her. "What did he say?" She wanted to hurry him along, to hear everything. But Manoah was not one who was quick to speak.

"He claims to be waiting for an opportunity to defeat the Philistines. He is staying with Delilah because he believes she is in contact with the lords of the Philistines and that she will lead him to destroy them. He is awaiting the right moment, and it has not yet come."

"Five years of waiting and he has done nothing but live with her?"

"And judge our people." Manoah gripped his staff but did not move from where he sat. "Raya, our son loves this woman. I asked him if he still keeps his Nazirite vows. His hair is still long, so I hold out hope that he has. He assured me that he is faithful to his vow. He is simply waiting on the right time. When it comes, he plans to kill every one of the Philistine lords. What could I say to that? It is a worthy goal and would deal a great blow to our enemies." He looked at her, his gaze assessing.

Raya twisted her hands in her lap. "Did he ask after me?" She dared not ask more. *Does he miss us? Does he love us too or just this foreign woman?*

"He did. He said to tell you that he thinks of you often and when he can get away, he will come home to visit. He claims that the time is close. We should soon hear of the destruction of the Philistine leaders. Once he accomplishes that, he will come home." Manoah's smile did not reach his eyes.

"You did not believe him," Raya said, touching his cheek. "If you did, your smile would be genuine, but it is guarded, my husband. Tell me...was our son telling the truth?" She desperately needed to know.

Manoah studied his staff, as though the answers to her questions were carved in its wood. "I believe him as much as I ever could. I think he speaks of what he wants to happen. I do not know if what he wants is what he will get. I do not know whether he is keeping the entire Nazirite vow or simply keeping his hair long. To live with this foreign woman is to break God's law, and I cannot make him see that this is not the way to defeat the Philistines."

"Did you try to tell him that?" She lifted her head, imploring.

He shook his head. "No. He is adamant, as always, and there is nothing we can do to make him choose our way over his. His love for this woman has blinded him, Raya. He might be able to take down these Philistine leaders like he thinks he can, or Delilah might be his undoing. We cannot know the future or whether God will continue to protect him." He took her hand and squeezed. "But our son lives and he misses us. Can we let that be enough for now? We can pray that he will soon come home."

Raya leaned her head against Manoah's chest. "I will try to let that be enough. I wish I could have gone with you and held him in my arms again. I would ask you to take me there so that

I can have that wish fulfilled. But I know my presence could upset his plans. If he is that close to destroying the lords of the land, then perhaps this is God's plan for him. Though I hardly think God would have chosen a foreign woman to help him accomplish such a daunting task."

He wouldn't do such a thing, would He? Yet God had filled Samson with power when his Philistine wife was killed. Was God using Samson's love for foreign women to harm the Philistines and weaken their army?

It made no sense to her, but the memory of the angel's words to her the day she first met him surfaced now. *He will begin to rescue Israel from the Philistines.*

The angel hadn't told her how he would do that, only that he would. It was up to her now to trust that God still guided her wayward son. Could a man believe and still disobey? The thought did not sit right with her, for it went against all she knew of God's law.

But as she rose from the stone seat with Manoah and began a slow walk toward home, she knew that her prayers had at last been answered. Her son was alive and still doing the work God had given him to do. And he missed her. Surely he loved them both. Surely he would keep his word and soon come home.

CHAPTER EIGHTEEN

Samson left the city gate of Beth-Shemesh as the sun began to descend in the west and took the well-worn path to Delilah's house in the valley. He had grown used to the routine these past years, and yet he still watched for bandits or wild animals as he made the trek to the woman's home.

He should have married her long ago, but despite his constant declarations of love to her, she pushed the idea of marriage away whenever the topic came from his lips.

"What do you have against marriage?" he'd asked, surprised that a woman would be so hesitant to have the added protection of a husband and sons. He would like for her to bear his son, but he'd hesitated to tell her that.

She had laughed at his question. "I have nothing against marriage for those who think they need it. But why do I need a man?" She cupped his cheek and smiled. "I have you, and you are more man than any woman can handle. To marry would only complicate things."

"Complicate what things?" She confused him with her ridiculous ideas, but he told himself she was a worshipper of Dagon, a foreigner who was bound to have confusing opinions.

"My life." She turned about and sauntered into the sitting area and sank with grace onto the cushions where she had often plied him with questions.

He followed her slowly. "I complicate your life?" He would not let her know that her words stung. He thought she loved him. How could love complicate things?

She lifted a hand to him. He took it and sat beside her. "Samson, my love, you are of Israel. I am a Philistine. Our people are enemies. Do you not recall what happened to your Philistine wife? I do not wish to end up the same way. If you stay with me, no one will care. But if we were to marry, we would make a bond that neither of our people would accept. Let's just leave things as they are, shall we?"

They'd dropped the subject after that, though he had not put it completely from his mind. Why did he stay with her if their relationship was not going to end well? By not wanting to marry, she also seemed to be clear that she did not wish to beget children. What woman did not long for sons as his mother had done? And why did Delilah continue to entertain visits at her neighbor's house with other men who had to have come from the rulers of the Philistines? Why had she begun entertaining them in her own house recently? Was she unfaithful to him with them? Did she love him at all?

But her allure kept him coming home to her each night. As he approached the house now, he saw the lamps in the windows and the outline of her form moving about the rooms.

Perhaps tonight he should broach the subject again. After the visit from his father, guilt had risen that he was breaking

God's laws by not marrying her. Was that why the subject had returned to his mind? He stopped at the door, the memory of his father's grief evident in his furrowed brow, and he knew his mother must be bitterly hurt by his absence. Why did he stay away from them? Why could he not stop himself from wanting to live with Delilah?

Because what he had told his father was true. He was certain she would lead him to the point where he could destroy the Philistine lords with one blow. Yes, that was the reason. His infatuation with Delilah was simply a means to an end. Perhaps he did not love her as much as he thought he did.

He opened the door and she greeted him.

"Samson, my darling, you are home at last." She wrapped her arms about his neck and kissed him until he lifted her into his arms and carried her to the couch.

"My, how you greet me. And here I thought you would fill my belly first." He pulled the combs from her hair, and she let him kiss her with abandon. But when he undid his robe, she sat up and gave a slight laugh.

"How ardent is my lover," she said, gently pushing on his chest. "Let us fill your belly first. I promise you will find plenty of time for this later."

She stood and pushed him back onto the couch, dismissing his desire to object with an alluring smile. She moved to the place where she kept the food and brought him a tray of meat and cheese, bread and olives and grapes. He looked at the food, briefly noting the cheese and grapes. She had never offered him grapes since the first time he had spent the night with her. And she knew he did not mix meat with cheese, so what was she trying to do? She knew he ate only food allowed in the law, and the meat was clean, which was good, but he always ate the cheeses at different meals than with his meat. And she knew grapes were forbidden to him.

He looked at her. "What's this?"

She sat opposite him and plopped a grape into her mouth. "I came upon a vineyard with ripe grapes today. You will try one, won't you?"

"You know that I don't eat meat and cheese together, nor has a grape ever touched my lips." That wasn't the whole truth, as he had been among the Philistines too long to resist sips of wine and raisin cakes now and then.

"Come now, Samson. You have tasted my wine. Surely a few grapes won't anger your god." She curled her lip in a pout, and he looked at the fruit, sudden longing filling him. He had been denied this taste his entire life. What would it hurt?

"You mock me, my love," he said, taking an olive, plopping it into his mouth and spitting the pit into a bowl.

She ate another grape, spitting the small seeds into the same bowl. She smiled, and they continued to eat in silence. She ate all of the types of food on the tray, while he avoided the grapes and cheese.

"Very well," she said at last when they had finished. "I see I cannot make you break your vow." She took the tray away and returned, curling into the crook of his arm. "But if you will not eat my food, then please stop putting me off and tell me what makes you so strong and what it would take to tie you up securely."

Samson pushed her away from him and searched her gaze. "Why do you ask me this again? If I did not know better, I would think you are looking for a way to destroy me, as your people would like to do."

She curled into him again and laughed. "How silly you are, my love. You live in my home and share my bed, yet you do not trust me. You suggest that we marry, yet you do not trust me." She sat up, pouting again. "How can you say you love me if you do not trust me? I only ask because I am testing you to see when you finally will. Perhaps then I will consider your thoughts of marriage." She traced her finger along his bearded jaw.

He closed his eyes, feeling the pull of her words. But he could not tell her. Despite everything, no matter how much he thought he loved her, she was right. He did not trust her.

He pulled her against him. He would tell her something to appease her. Yes. Play her little game. Perhaps she would soon tire of asking once she realized that he could not be tempted to give up his secret.

He leaned against her and whispered in her ear. "If I were tied up with seven new bowstrings that have not yet been dried, I would become as weak as anyone else."

She fairly purred against him, and he pulled her into his arms, intending to finish what he had begun when he first arrived. She turned toward him, and as the lamps flickered in the windows at the blackness of night, she did not disappoint him.

A week passed, and Samson continued his routine of judging Israel and returning home to Delilah. She made no more mention of her question, and he breathed a sigh of relief that perhaps by telling her what he did, she would forget about caring what he kept from her.

He returned home later than usual that night and found that Delilah had left food out for him, but she was already asleep in their bed. Was she ill? It was not like her to take to bed before his return. He stepped into the room, thinking to wake her, but her even breathing and peaceful expression made him pause. He could spend one night by himself, couldn't he?

He left the sleeping chamber and took the food to the sitting area and ate in silence. He drank from the skin of goat's milk, reminded of the way his mother had always made sure he had plenty of food and drink of every kind he was allowed to eat. He missed her pistachio cakes and the date pastries that no one could make as well as his imma.

Longing to see her again surfaced, and he could not stop the image of her loving look or the way she held him in her strong arms. Childhood memories also surfaced, and he realized how much he must have hurt her by staying away so much of his adult life. He had passed his thirty-sixth birthday. Why had he kept his distance? Why not just go home for a visit?

He pushed the food away, suddenly no longer hungry. He should get up and go now. Delilah could wonder where he'd gone, but she would welcome him back again. She was predictable in that regard. Surely she would understand his need to please Imma. Hadn't he promised his father he would do that very thing?

But he had promised other things as well—was sure that by now he would have done more to hurt the Philistines than he had. Delilah had done nothing yet to give him insight into her strange visitors, even when he asked. Perhaps he should sit and wait for them to enter the neighbor's house and then kill them all. It wouldn't be as big as a war, but perhaps his brothers in Israel would join him in a battle against them if he could begin there.

He turned the idea over in his mind. He wouldn't walk to Zorah tonight. He needed daylight to see the paths. And it wasn't like the Philistines were about to visit Delilah while he slept.

He sat in indecision, wondering why his life suddenly felt so confusing. He rose and slipped quietly into bed then waited for sleep to come. Delilah's even breathing relaxed him as he concentrated on the quiet sound and slowly drifted off to sleep. He dreamed of Zorah and his childhood and the many times he had pouted as a child against the vow.

Why was it so hard to do what he had been called to do? And yet he chafed and twisted even in his dreams until it felt as though he were running far away to a place he did not recognize.

A loud shout jolted him, and he bolted upright, nearly falling off the edge of the bed when he found his arms and feet bound.

"Samson!" Delilah's voice pulled him out of his stupor. "The Philistines have come to capture you!" He blinked hard and twisted his head to better see the bowstrings holding him captive. Exactly as he had told her he could be restrained.

He looked into the dimly lit room, saw the shadows of men in the next room, and snapped the bowstrings as though they had turned to ash, burned in a fire. He tossed them aside and stood. The men in the other room fled. Samson grabbed his staff and ran after them.

But Delilah stood in his way.

"Get out of my way," he growled, nearly shoving her aside.

She placed a hand on his chest. "Samson. Do not go after them. It was only a test. They are long gone by now anyway."

"You mean gone to the neighbor's house to cower until the light of day." He glared at her. "Let me go and kill them."

Her eyes went wide. "You would do that? When we were only playing a game with you?" Hurt filled her expression.

He felt the ire in his blood slowly cool. "A game? You would risk my life in a game?"

She shrugged. "You did not trust me. I wanted to see if you had."

He released a deep sigh. Warring thoughts urged him to go after the Philistines, while the others called him to forget the matter and take her to bed. Or maybe he should just leave.

"No more games," he said sternly. He glanced at the door. Had those men truly left? Could he trust her enough to go back to sleep? But one touch and he could destroy any threat. Despite her motives, he was safe. God was with him. Yes. He breathed in again. God *was* with him. He turned and left her side to return to the bed. He would deal with her in the morning.

CHAPTER NINETEEN

Raya woke with a start, the dream of Samson too vivid, too real. She blinked hard, trying to clear her head. *Samson. Oh my son.* He'd been bound and carried off by the Philistines. Yet how could that be? He was too strong to be bound. Up until now he had defeated every foe.

And hadn't Manoah just spoken to him a month past? He'd been well, planned to visit them soon, he'd said. He was going to defeat the lords of the Philistines.

She turned, aware that Manoah still slept at her side, but she could no longer lie still. She rose carefully and moved to the window, looking into the blackness of night. A chill curled her toes on the stone floor, and she reached for her cloak to wrap about her.

It was a simple dream. That's all. And yet…was God warning her of the future? Of Samson's coming fate? If He was, what could she possibly do about it?

She walked from the room into the main sitting area, careful to keep from making a sound. Barefoot, she moved into the courtyard and looked up at the multitude of stars. Silence fell over the house, and the cool air nipped at her bare legs.

She lifted her gaze, her heartbeat picking up its pace as it had that moment the dream had awakened her. What did it mean? *Why did I dream like this?* Her people had always put significance on certain dreams, though few would consider themselves a prophet or prophetess who might hear from the Lord in this way.

Perhaps she had eaten too much with the evening meal.

She stood staring at the heavens, when the door creaked open and Manoah joined her, resting his hand on her shoulder.

"Raya. What troubles you? You will catch a chill out here." He worried overmuch about her, but besides Samson, whom else did he have to care or worry over?

"I had a dream," she said softly. "Of Samson." She looked into his eyes, his form growing more visible in the moonlight.

"Tell me." He took her hand and squeezed.

"He was bound and taken captive by the Philistines." Tears filled her eyes. "He has never been able to be captured. Is this a sign from the Lord?"

Manoah pulled her close, and she rested her head on his chest. "I cannot say whether your dream is from the Lord or not, Raya. If it comes to pass, then we will know it was true."

She shivered against him. "I don't want it to come true."

"I know. Neither do I. But Samson is a grown man, and he is doing what he thinks is right. Whether he is living in obedience to the Lord and the Lord allows him to be captured by the Philistines is only something our God knows. We cannot know the future, even in our dreams." He stroked her head and she breathed in his scent, calmed by his words.

He was right. It was just a dream. She couldn't know the future, and if Samson was in danger of capture, surely God would be with him. Surely God would not abandon the child He had claimed since before his birth.

"Let's try to get some sleep," Manoah whispered against her ear. "Dawn will be here too soon, and tomorrow will see enough trouble of its own. Let's not add to it by our worries." He led her gently back into the house, and she followed in silence, hoping no one else in the house had been awakened by their voices or footfalls.

She hung her robe on the hook again and settled beneath the covers next to Manoah. She would not worry. Samson would be fine. One day he would take down the Philistines and break their hold over Israel. She just needed to be patient until he could accomplish his purpose. But she prayed for him before sleep could claim her, just the same.

"You've been making fun of me and telling me lies!" Delilah shouted the following week, after Samson was certain she had put the matter of his strength behind them. What was wrong with her? "Please," she pleaded, "tell me how you can be tied up securely."

The day had not gone well, and he was still nursing anger at one of the Israelite men who had come to him to judge a case between him and the head of his family. The matter should not have been Samson's to consider. The head of the family should have made the decision and his decision been accepted as final. But the younger man bore a grudge against this older brother who had inherited the authority of his clan when their father died. He didn't appreciate such petty needs. Who was he to tell them what to do?

Sometimes he hated this mantle God had put upon him. And now he stared at this woman who would not let such a foolish request go. He lifted his eyes to the ceiling, wishing he were outside gazing up at the sky. Perhaps he could make sense of her if God would explain why she kept asking such things.

But didn't he know? She, like every other Philistine, wanted to see him destroyed. His gut told him it was true, but his heart balked at the idea. No. Impossible. He loved her. She was still playing with him. Even her anger was simply her way of upping the stakes of the game.

He closed the door that had remained open until this moment. "All right," he said, walking over to the couch and lowering his large body to the deep cushions. "I will tell you."

She moved closer, dark eyes wide with interest.

"If I were tied up with brand-new ropes that had never been used, I would become as weak as anyone else." He held her gaze until he was certain she believed him.

She nestled beside him. "Thank you," she said. "Though I hope you are not toying with me again."

"Why would you think that?" He would have laughed, but her sincere tone made him pause. She meant every word. The thought sent a knot to the pit of his gut. This was no game with her. Of course it was. No, it wasn't.

He continued to argue with himself throughout the evening meal, and as he lay down beside her, he wondered if he would awaken to her frantic call again. But morning dawned and he rose without incident.

She was just testing him, he told himself over and over, yet not believing a single word.

Two nights later, Samson could finally relax. Delilah smiled at him as usual and their conversation was of her gardening and keeping the house, while he told her of the people he had judged in Beth-Shemesh. Life could be normal again. He drew in a breath and slowly released it. While she prepared for bed, he lay down, thinking to wait for her, but his eyes grew heavy, and he fought the desire for sleep.

Footsteps, obviously those of Delilah, sounded in the next room, but he did not look to see her enter. She would rouse him when she was ready, and he would take her into his arms.

The thought lingered as he rolled to his side.

"Samson!" He jolted awake at her voice. "The Philistines have come to capture you!" New ropes held his arms to the wood bedframe, restricting his movement. He snapped them with ease and jumped from the bed.

"How long will you try to deceive me, woman?" His voice rang in the house and echoed beyond the walls.

Delilah appeared, blocking his way from the sleeping area, though they both knew she was no match for him. Footsteps sounded louder now, and Samson knew she'd had men waiting again to capture him. Why did he put up with her?

"You lied to me," she said, her tone caustic. "How can I ever trust you again?" She turned away from him, and for a moment he wondered if she would ask him to leave, but deep down he knew she wanted him there. Wanted to find the secret of his strength no matter the cost to either of them.

Were they paying her to do this? Or did she hate him as much as he thought she must?

He stormed out of the house and headed for the hills. Maybe it was time he went home.

CHAPTER TWENTY

R aya heard him before she caught sight of him lumbering toward their house. "Samson!" She called his name and jumped up from her work of the meal preparation and ran down the road to meet him. "Samson! My son. You are home!" She did not stop until he caught her into his arms and lifted her off her feet.

"Imma." He held her close and buried his head against her hair, kissing her cheek. "It is so good to see you." He held her at arm's length. "I am sorry I stayed away so long."

Raya searched his face even as she cupped his cheek. "It is of no consequence at all. You are home now and that is what matters." She smiled, joy bubbling within her. Her boy was home! How light her heart felt.

"Is Abba here or out in the fields?" He glanced beyond her toward the sheep pens. He released his hold on her but placed one arm about her shoulders as they walked.

"He is in the fields. Come, he will be happy to see you too." She turned him toward the area where Manoah said he would take the sheep, and Samson seemed to shorten his long strides to keep her pace.

"How have you been?" Raya asked as they stepped off the path to walk through the grassy fields where wildflowers waved in the slight breeze.

"I am well," he said, his voice holding a hint of frustration. "I have been judging Israel in Beth-Shemesh and staying in the Valley of Sorek." He did not mention Delilah, and Raya debated with herself whether or not she should ask about the woman.

"Isn't the Valley of Sorek part of Philistine territory? Do Israelites have homes there? I have never seen it." She told herself she wasn't prying, but one glance at him and the stiff way he set his jaw and she knew he did not like the question.

"I know of no Israelite homes in the area. I am living with a Philistine." He did not specify more, and she sensed he would not.

"Are you happy, my son? Has God given you opportunity to fight our enemies as you once did?" She linked her arm through his, and he patted her hand.

"I am happy, Imma. You do not need to worry about me. I am waiting for the right time, but I believe God is close to giving the Philistine leaders into my hands. When that happens, I hope my brothers in Israel will take up the fight against them." He sounded sure, and she nodded in silence.

Manoah appeared in the distance, and she waved to him with her free hand. "There he is." She released Samson as he began a short jog to reach his father. Raya hurried to keep up, not wanting to miss a word they said to each other. Just hearing Samson's voice was like water to the thirsty.

Samson embraced Manoah and kissed each cheek. Raya breathed heavily as she finally reached them.

"So you are home, my son," Manoah said, smiling. "Does this mean you have defeated the lords of the Philistines as you'd hoped?"

Samson shook his head. "Not yet." He looked at his feet as though the admission brought shame. "I have been waiting on Delilah's help, but she is most confusing." His admission warmed Raya's heart. For him to be honest with them was rare.

"How so?" Manoah asked, leaning on his staff.

"She keeps trying to find out the secret of my strength. I tell her something that isn't true. She tries to use it against me, while men are waiting to capture me as I sleep. She won't stop asking and is most put out with me."

"Perhaps you should stay away from her then," Raya said, alarmed that this woman would do such a thing and worse, that Samson would continue to let her.

Samson lifted his head, his expression sorrowful. "I can't, Imma. I love her. She keeps drawing me back, and I can't stop from returning. But this last time, I left. If I spend time with you both, I will be able to put up with her taunts. She needs to think she has lost me. Perhaps then she will stop asking."

Manoah stroked his beard, his look thoughtful. "Do you think you will be tempted to tell her the truth?" His gaze held Samson's, probing.

Samson's sure look did not waver for a long moment, but at last he glanced away. "I don't know, Abba. I'm not sure I have what it takes to put up with her constant nagging."

"Then you should definitely stay away from her, Samson," Raya said, fear rising within her. "I dreamed that the Philistines captured you. What if Delilah succeeds in tempting you and you are caught? How will you escape then?" She hadn't planned to tell him her dream, but fear moved through her like a living thing.

Samson turned to her. "You dreamed of me, Imma?"

She nodded. "It frightened me."

He regarded her then studied the dirt at his feet again. "I won't tell her the truth, Imma. Your dream was just a dream. You worry about me too much." His voice hardened ever so slightly, and the brief moment of his honesty seemed to evaporate.

"Let us talk of other things," he said, glancing at the flock grazing nearby.

They began a slow walk toward home though there were still many hours of daylight left, Manoah calling the sheep to follow.

"Tell me how you both have been," Samson said, changing his tone to a lighter one. Their conversation would be less honest now, for Samson had already stiffened against their suggestions. Raya's heart sank as they walked and Manoah told Samson about the crops and the sheep.

Had she said too much? Given unwanted advice? Why was this son so stubborn? Did he really think himself stronger than a woman he loved? Philistine women had been a bane to him more than once before Delilah. What if she wore him down and he couldn't stop himself from telling her everything?

What if he did tell her about his vow and all that it entailed? Would that even matter? It was God who worked within him far more than any adherence to his vow. If he broke his vow...that didn't mean God would leave him. Did it? Did he believe that?

She struggled with her thoughts as she listened to her husband and son speak of normal life—of caring for their home and judging Israel. Things she cared about because they mattered to her men. But she wished with all of her heart that her son would trust her with his heart and come to see how vulnerable he could be. Why was he so blind to his own weakness? And why did he shut out any advice she gave him?

But as they entered the house and later ate with the family, who all welcomed Samson home, she pushed her fears aside. Samson might return to Delilah before she had a chance to enjoy him very long, and she would not waste a moment more worrying over him. She would pray, but she would enjoy this unexpected visit and embed it in her memory. Once he left, she had no promise that she would ever see him again. That thought alone troubled her most.

Samson stayed less than a week, and Raya watched Manoah head to the fields again, the sheep straggling behind, Elead at his side. She moved into the courtyard to join the women, trying to set her mind to the tasks at hand and put aside the grief of missing her son. He could have stayed with them and brought a wife home to live, but she had a feeling deep down that this was not his fate. He had a different calling and a different stubborn streak than most of the members of Manoah's household.

A sigh lifted her chest. Life would go back to normal, as it had been these many years of Samson's absence, and she must accept it. She would do all she could to make Manoah's years with her the best they could be.

Talia joined her as Raya pulled a bag of pistachios from a shelf and began to shell them. She would make Manoah's favorite pastry to add to the meal. Give him something to smile over, for she knew Samson's departure bothered him more than he would ever admit.

"Perhaps he will return again soon," Talia said, helping her with the shelling. "It was good to see him again. He has grown taller and stronger, if that is possible."

Raya met Talia's gaze and smiled. "It *was* good to see him. I do hope he returns more often now, but his plans against the Philistines may prevent him from doing that."

"Do you really think he can take out all of the Philistine lords at once?" The question was sincere, Raya knew, but she had no honest answer.

"I don't know. I hope so. I hope he takes them down before they capture him." She lowered her voice, unable to stem the tide of emotion rising within her again.

Talia touched Raya's hand. "Don't think like that. We will pray Samson does what he believes he can do. We can't fear the worst or we will live in constant worry."

Raya nodded. "You are right," she told Talia. "We will keep praying for his safety and trust that all will be well."

"That's a good attitude to keep," Talia said. They shared a smile and Raya's heart felt lighter by the encouragement.

All would turn out better than she thought. Better than her dream. She would simply choose to believe it. If she didn't believe it, she would live in misery, and that was not a way she wanted to spend her life.

The pastries were baking in the clay oven when shouts were heard coming from the fields where Manoah and Elead had gone that morning. Amichai and Chaim raced toward the house, calling Raya and Talia.

"Aunt Raya, Imma, you must come at once!" They stopped in the courtyard, bent over and out of breath, hands on their knees.

"What happened?" Raya jumped up, followed by not only Talia but also the rest of the women.

"The Philistines—a few of their raiders—wandered into our fields and caught us unaware. They shot at us with their arrows."

Raya's heart leapt then pounded as though it would explode in her chest. "Where are Manoah and Elead?"

"You must come," Chaim repeated.

The women grabbed their cloaks and baskets of herbs and raced after Raya's nephews. "You must tell us what happened," Raya insisted as they ran. "Please."

Chaim came alongside Raya and his mother. "Both men are hurt. We can carry them to the house, but we thought you might be able to bind their wounds first."

"They're over here!" Amichai called, having raced ahead of the others. He waved even as he knelt beside the two men.

Raya hurried to Manoah's side and fell to her knees. "Manoah!" She bent close to listen to his breathing. His eyes fluttered open, but she could see the arrow sticking out of his leg and blood pooling beneath him on the ground. She could barely look at the wound, and she searched the rest of his body first to be sure it was the only place he'd been hurt.

"Raya," he rasped, reaching for her hand, "it is my bad leg they shot."

She nodded, having realized the obvious the moment she saw the stick protruding from him. She moved to give it a closer look. "Chaim," she called.

Her nephew came quickly, as Amichai stayed with Talia to help Elead, who had also been hit.

"Can you pull it out?" She hated to ask, for she had no idea what damage an arrow could do once it was pulled from a body. It could tear parts internal that would make him bleed more or damage more.

Chaim knelt opposite her and examined his uncle. He looked at Manoah. "If I help you, Uncle, do you think you can walk?"

Manoah groaned but slowly nodded. "If you are strong enough to half carry me."

"I will help hold up his other side. We will both carry him." She glanced at Chaim, who nodded his assent.

"I think we would do well to wait to cut it out after he is home. I thought you might bind it to his leg, though, so it doesn't move as we get him home."

The herbs would do little good until they pulled it out, but binding the leg would help some. She hoped. She pulled linen strips from her basket and quickly draped them over the leg, while Chaim lifted the leg so she could go over and under. Manoah winced but did not cry out.

"How is Elead?" Raya asked Chaim as she worked.

Chaim glanced behind him then turned to face her. "Much the same as Uncle Manoah."

She finished the work and tied off the binding. She glanced at the other women working on Elead, who did not seem as responsive as Manoah. Were they injured the same?

"Do you think you are ready, my husband?" she asked, anxious to get him home, longing to send for Samson to help, but worried that neither of them would be able to help Manoah if infection set in.

"I think I'm ready." He pushed up on his elbows, and Chaim took hold of him and lifted him to his feet. Manoah cried out but quickly quieted. Raya handed him his walking stick and braced his other side. He managed to keep his wounded leg from touching the ground most of the way.

"Are the others coming?" Manoah asked, his tone worried but strained, obviously hiding his pain.

Raya glanced behind her. Elead had not been moved, and Talia, Karmela, Amichai, and the other women so surrounded him that she could barely see him. "Not yet," she said, turning back to watch where she stepped.

The walk was slow going, but they approached the house with no sign of the others yet following. She shared a look with Chaim behind Manoah's back. His expression held worry, and she wanted to send him to his father, but she needed his help to remove the arrow.

"If you can find a way to take this out of his leg, you can return to help your father. I can manage from there."

They entered her bedchamber and laid Manoah among the cushions of the bed. Chaim left her to find a tool to help him pull the arrow from Manoah's leg while she doused a linen rag in spiced wine. She held it to him and let him sip on it.

Chaim returned and Raya had laid a pile of linens beneath the wound to catch the blood and bind his leg with herbs. Why had this happened to him? *Adonai?* Why had He allowed her family to be hurt more than they already had been by the Philistines? Samson had not killed any of them in recent years, if what he said was true, so why this? Why now?

Her thoughts were cut short at her husband's screams as Chaim pulled the arrow from his leg. Despite his efforts to be gentle, the pointed barb tore the skin and much beneath it. Raya closed her eyes then opened them and poured fresh water drawn that morning over the wound and quickly mixed a poultice of herbs and bound it fast. Manoah passed out from the pain, a relief to him. But the whole ordeal felt like a fist to Raya's middle.

"I need to help my father," Chaim said, interrupting her thoughts.

"Yes, of course." She watched him rush off, struck by the sudden silence. Why were they taking so long to bring Elead home? His wounds must have been worse. How much worse? But she dared not go where her thoughts wanted to take her. All she could focus on now was Manoah and somehow sending word to Samson.

CHAPTER TWENTY-ONE

"You've been making fun of me and telling me lies!" Delilah met Samson at the door, hands on her hips.

"Greetings to you as well." He scowled at her anger, questioning his sanity for returning. Why did he keep putting up with this woman?

"Tell me how you can be tied up securely." Her insistence had grown bolder. He had been gone nearly a week and just returned from judging Israel when he finally entered her house again—to this?

"Delilah, I grow weary of you asking the same question. Why should I tell you? I cannot trust you."

"Then why do you come back to me? You know this is what I want from you." She stared at him, all attempt at seduction gone.

He heaved a sigh as he pushed past her into the room. "Give me something to eat and I will tell you." He wouldn't. And he sensed that she knew it. Was she simply unable to stop herself from asking? Or was she after the coins she had surely been promised? Was he of so little value to her that she would sell him to her people?

"Sit down. I've made your favorite stew." Her tone softened then, and she went to retrieve the bread and lentil stew.

She ate with him then put the food away and settled beside him as usual. "Now tell me," she insisted.

"Do you already have men waiting to capture me in the next room?" His tone held the scorn he felt.

She looked offended. "Do you trust me so little?"

"Yes."

She glanced toward an adjacent room. "Go and see for yourself then."

He held her gaze. "All right." He stood and walked to the room, knowing he would find it empty. She would not be so foolish as to have men waiting when she didn't have anything to tell them. But he looked just the same.

"Satisfied?" she asked once he sat down again.

"For now." He leaned his head against the cushions, suddenly weary of his life. What use was it to have strength when he could do so little with it? He had not conquered a single Philistine city or killed a single one of their leaders. Was this really what God wanted of him? Perhaps he had been misguided all of these years. Had his mother truly seen an angel of the Lord? Or was it *her* desire that he remain a Nazirite? If this was all because of his parents' wishes and not of God's at all, then why was he so worried about secrets and judging his people? He could live life as he wanted to—especially if none of what he'd been taught was really true.

The thought sent a fist-like knot to his gut, and he closed his eyes against the temptation to tell her everything. What if his whole life had been built on the imaginings of his mother? Imma had tried so hard to control him, to keep him from doing anything to break his vow. But when he'd killed the lion and touched the corpse for the honey, nothing bad had happened to him. When he'd sipped the wine at Philistine feasts, nothing had changed. So why should he never cut his hair? Why should he care about following God's laws at all?

The sensation of falling came over him, and for the first time in his life he felt unsteady and about to lose himself to a force too great for him to ignore.

"Samson?" Delilah touched his arm, startling him. "Are you going to tell me?"

Suddenly, he could not give in to her, despite the doubts now assailing him. He'd been swept away by them, and he still felt adrift on a sea of raw emotions and shaky fear. "If you were to weave the seven braids of my hair into the fabric on your loom and tighten it with the loom shuttle, I would become as weak as anyone else."

He'd come close. He'd mentioned his hair, as he never had before. But weaving it into a loom wouldn't cut the braids, would it? If it did and he lost his strength, then he would know how mistaken he'd been. His strength either came from God or it was his own.

And for the first time in his life, he wanted to know. Was the strength his, or did the Spirit of God truly give him power beyond himself when he needed it? He'd been able to do impossible feats, but how did he really know those things came from God?

Maybe telling Delilah the truth would answer that question once and for all. But he wasn't yet willing to tell her. His own doubts were too close to the surface. And he wasn't sure he trusted himself.

Elead was finally carried to the house, but when Raya left Manoah's side for a moment to see how he fared, she saw the ashen look on Talia's face and one look at her brother-in-law told her the chances of him living were worse than Manoah's.

"The arrow caught him in the middle," Talia said. "He is taller than Manoah, or their aim was higher, and I fear the damage is worse." Tears filled her eyes and she swallowed, unable to speak.

Raya held her close and led her to a chair. Karmela moved about the room replacing poultices as she'd done for Manoah once or twice already, but Elead did not awaken, while Manoah had begun to speak a few words. Neither man was yet safe from infection, but Raya feared Elead could die of his wounds.

"I can't lose him, Raya," Talia whispered. "What will I do without him?" She rested her head on Raya's shoulder.

"You have Amichai and Chaim and the girls and all of us. And you do not yet know if God will take him to Sheol. Do not yet fret, my sister. Wait and see. And pray." Raya's words felt hollow, but she said them just the same.

"I've done nothing but pray. I see no change in him." She sat back against the seat, her shoulders slumped. "I have sent Chaim to get Samson for you."

Raya lifted a brow. "You did?" She hadn't expected either boy to leave his father's side.

"You need your son. Amichai has been here for me. Chaim will return soon."

Raya nodded. Samson would come. But what would he do to the Philistines once he saw what they had done to his father and uncle? She shuddered, wondering, uncertain.

"You should get some rest," Raya said, touching Talia's arm.

Talia shook her head. "I will rest near him at night. I cannot rest well, knowing that he might be lingering between this world and the next. He has not spoken since we found him."

Raya looked at Elead, stricken by the sallow hue of his skin. The arrow had done much damage. It was surprising he had lived after the blow, but both men still breathed. Would God heal them both?

Raya silently prayed as much, but sometimes her prayers were mere groans, matching the ones coming from Manoah. "I must return to Manoah," she said, the thought of him making her long to make sure nothing had changed.

Talia nodded. "Thank you. Go to him. May God be gracious to us both."

Raya merely nodded. Nothing else could be said.

Raya woke in the middle of the night to the sounds of shouting. She jumped up, checked on Manoah, who still slept, and ran to the room where the noise was coming from. Talia sat on the floor rocking back and forth, weeping, groaning. Amichai and her daughters-in-law surrounded the bed of their father, whose still form told Raya he had breathed his last and even now had gone the way of all the earth.

"I've sent a servant for Chaim, Imma. He will come quickly." Amichai sat beside his mother, one arm about her shoulders.

Talia merely rocked and groaned. Raya knelt on her other side and touched her knee. "I'm so sorry, my sister." Tears filled her eyes and she looked on her once vibrant brother-in-law, stricken. "When did he pass?" When they'd gone to sleep, he still breathed. Had Talia remained awake with him through the night, or did she just somehow know?

"I found him, Aunt Raya." Amichai glanced at her above Talia's head. "I came to check when I woke with a start. Imma was sleeping on the floor nearby. I sent for Chaim before I woke her."

Raya nodded her thanks. Had Chaim gotten to Beth-Shemesh or the Valley of Sorek or wherever he might find Samson before the servant would reach him? Or would Samson hear the news from a servant?

"Will the servant go on and tell Samson?" She held Amichai's gaze. "He should be here for his uncle."

Amichai's expression held confusion, as though he couldn't remember exactly what he had told the servant. "I'm sorry, Aunt Raya. I cannot remember what was said other than to find Chaim. If he returns with Chaim, we will send him back to find Samson."

She nodded again and turned her attention to Talia. Her sister-in-law would be of no help to them in this condition, and they must prepare the body for burial. She faced Amichai again. "Take your mother to the sitting room. Send for Karmela and Ariel—they might not have heard the shouts. We must prepare the body. Once Chaim returns, your father must be placed in the cave with his fathers."

She spoke, but her words sounded like they were coming from someone else. She slowly stood and helped Talia to her feet. "I want to help," Talia said, but Raya shook her head.

"It would not be fitting, my sister. Let Karmela and I do this for you. Go and rest until he is ready." She turned to the wives of Talia's sons. "Find plenty of linen wrappings. One of you go and ask Karmela to bring the spices. Amichai, we will need a bier. Can you get one built? Rouse Ariel and the other men to help you."

Amichai released a breath as though he were relieved that she was giving them direction. She wasn't used to taking charge like this, but she could think of no better way to show her support for her family. Manoah still slept, and she doubted he would be able to travel to the cave for his brother.

Karmela entered the room as Amichai led Talia out. "I didn't hear the commotion. I am sorry. When did this happen?"

"Only a few moments ago. Amichai found him. As if he woke out of a sound sleep for that very purpose." Raya moved to the opposite side of the bed where Karmela stood, both of them looking down at Elead, so peaceful, so ashen and cold.

"We must wash him first then sprinkle him with spices then wrap him in the linens." Karmela spoke, her voice stoic, as one who recites words without feeling. "It's been some time since we had to do this." She glanced at Raya.

"Not since their mother and father sixteen years ago." Raya felt a pang of loss all over again. She missed her mother-in-law.

"It's not right. What happened is not right." Karmela turned to get the spices, shaking her head.

Raya left the room to retrieve the jar of water and cloths to wash his body. The task ahead of them sent a chill down her spine. What would Samson do once he heard? Would this be the start of a war with the Philistines? Would Samson come back so soon?

She slipped into her room to check on Manoah. His eyes opened at her approach. "What happened? I heard many voices."

She sighed, wishing she could have kept the news from him longer, knowing she couldn't. "It is your brother," she said, kneeling at his side. "He has passed this night into Sheol." She touched his arm, the tears returning, despite her attempts to keep them at bay. She would weep once they had completed their tasks. Right now was not the time.

"This night?" He looked beyond her, a faraway expression in his eyes.

"Yes. Only a few moments ago. We are getting ready to prepare his body for the burial cave." She cupped his cheek and he met her gaze. "I don't want you to worry if you cannot come. You need to rest lest your wounds become infected. We cannot lose you both."

He seemed to ponder her words, even as he pushed himself into a sitting position. "I will come," he said. "When you are ready to go, have servants help me, and I will come."

The thought worried her. He wasn't strong enough for such a long walk to the caves outside of their city. Perhaps if he rode a donkey. "Let me talk to Amichai. We will work out something for you, but right now you must promise me that you will rest."

He nodded, slowly lowering himself back onto the mat. Tears slipped from his eyes and wet the cushions beneath his head. He closed his eyes, as if in obedience to her, and she waited a moment more until he seemed to be resting as she'd suggested. She turned and went to retrieve the water and cloths, praying that she would not soon be doing this same task for Manoah as well.

Samson slept peacefully for a change, satisfied that Delilah was worth the frustration. She certainly knew how to please a man. He'd never met a woman like her, and even in his dreams, he saw her at his side, bearing his children. If dreams came true, he hoped his were the ones that did so and not his mother's. His thoughts moved in and out of wild images, seeing in his mind's eye memories mixed with strange things and people he'd met, none of it making any sense. It felt so real, as though he could touch the child Delilah would soon bear him. She stood before him, her belly protruding with the evidence of their love.

"Samson!" Her shout jolted him out of the dream. "The Philistines have come to capture you!" He twisted this way and that, feeling the braids of his hair caught in the loom shuttle.

He blinked hard, the dream a misty memory. He pulled his hair out of the loom, shoving it away from the fabric, and stood.

"Woman, I swear to you, I will leave you for good if you do not stop this!" Anger stirred within him and he longed to rip something apart or destroy her house—something.

Delilah stepped slowly closer and placed a hand on his chest, her lower lip curled in her typical pout. She actually looked beautiful to him even when she pouted, but he held back the smile he felt trying to replace his anger.

"How can you tell me 'I love you' when you don't share your secrets with me? You've made fun of me three times now, and you still haven't told me what makes you so strong!"

He placed both hands on the sides of her head. "And I'm not going to tell you." He softened his tone, despite the anger still seething beneath the surface. "Stop asking me, or I mean it. I will leave you and find another way to destroy your people, since you seem so bent on destroying me. Don't think I won't."

She took a step back at that and seemed smaller to him all of a sudden. Perhaps she was not as tough as she attempted to be. "If you loved me, like you say you do, you would tell me."

"I love you, dear woman, but I do not trust a word you say. How I can love you is a mystery to me. But you and I both know that the truth is something you cannot keep to yourself." He crossed his arms over his chest. "Now come to bed with me and stop this nonsense." He took her arm and pulled her into the sleeping room, away from the loom and anything else she might try to use against him.

She followed in seeming meekness, but as he lay beside her, facing her, he dared not close his eyes, even when he heard her soft snoring. He wasn't afraid she could conquer him when he told her lies. But the doubts that had surfaced at her last attempt to pull the truth from him had not left him. He'd stopped going to Beth-Shemesh to judge Israel and roamed the hills for days instead, questioning everything he'd ever been taught.

Was God truly with him? Did it matter? He'd never actually heard God speak. Only once or twice had God answered a prayer he'd prayed, one when he had desperately needed water, and a few times he thought the strength to kill the Philistines must be coming from somewhere beyond him. But now? Now he could not decide what was truth or lie. Was anything real? Did God exist at all? His heart thudded hard with not knowing, with doubt. How was he supposed to discern and know if God was real for himself? Without the constant memory of his parents' insistence he keep this vow?

And how was he going to deal with Delilah? His frustration grew and ever-increasing weariness filled him because of this nagging woman. How long would he put up with her? Could he truly walk away and let her go?

Maybe giving in to her would put an end to all of this and they could live in peace. Have the child he'd dreamed of. Be the husband to her he longed to be.

But she did not want a husband or child, and somewhere deep in his gut he knew his dreams were impossible. Irritated with his thoughts, he at last rose from the bed, knowing that sleep would not come, and left the house. He needed to clear his head, but he wasn't sure how to do that.

He couldn't go home again, and he wasn't sure he could stay here. He could live in the hills but for how long? He didn't like being alone. He needed a woman at his side. And he felt as though he had lost his life's purpose. He needed a reason for being. Was it truly to destroy the Philistines and live this restrictive life?

Or could he set this all aside and have something better? Something less burdensome? He longed to ask his father the question but knew his father would simply tell him to trust God. And it was God whom he questioned most.

PART FIVE

Finally, Samson shared his secret with her.... So the Philistines captured him and gouged out his eyes. They took him to Gaza, where he was bound with bronze chains and forced to grind grain in the prison.

But before long, his hair began to grow back.

—Judges 16:17, 21–22 (NLT)

CHAPTER TWENTY-TWO

Chaim returned home before dawn with the servant in tow. Raya's heart sank when she realized that they had not found Samson. He could not be reached in time to lay his uncle to rest. And his father needed him too, but she dare not send anyone for him until Elead lay with his fathers.

The day dragged on even though the women barely stopped to rest or eat. Before sunset, the family had gathered around a new bier and Elead's body was wrapped in linens atop it. Manoah, looking ashen, a blanket covering his legs, sat on a donkey led by one of the servants as the group slowly made its way through the city to the caves lining the hills outside of it. Mourners joined them as they walked, weeping loudly as the line grew long.

Raya walked beside Manoah, her heart heavy with missing Samson. He should be here for this. How would he react when he heard of his uncle's death after the fact? But she couldn't blame Chaim for not finding him. He'd gone to Beth-Shemesh, but Samson had not been in his usual place judging Israel. No one had seen him in days, and Raya couldn't stop the worry that gnawed at her. Had her dream come true and the Philistines captured him?

The thoughts troubled her, adding to the grief she bore every time she glanced at Talia. What would they do without Elead? He'd been Manoah's closest friend, more so than Ariel was. But what would happen if they lost Manoah too?

They slowly made their way toward the caves in the hills, nearly a half-day's walk from the city.

"How are you feeling?" Raya asked Manoah. It was the third time she had asked him that morning, but she could not stop the concern she felt every time she looked at him.

"The same as I was the last time you asked me," he said, attempting a smile. His hair and beard were unkempt despite her attempts to wash him and comb through the tangles. Since the incident, it had taken enough of his strength just to let them change the poultices and give him broth to nourish him.

"I fear for you." She touched his arm as she walked beside him.

"The donkey is doing all of the work. I'm fine, Raya." She saw the slight wince in his eyes and knew he had not told her the whole truth.

"When we return, I will send someone to find Samson. He should be here for you, if not for your brother." How anyone would find her son, she did not know, but if she could go herself, she would. *Samson, where are you?* But even her prayers had yielded no answer, not even a feeling of peace in her heart.

She looked up as the line of mourners came to a stop and realized they had at last reached the burial caves. Elead's sons and nephews rolled the heavy stone away. Ariel said a few words

Raya barely heard, and at last the men carried Elead's body into the tomb.

A piercing wail came from Talia as the men returned without Elead's body and rolled the stone back into place. She fell to her knees and buried her face in the dust.

Raya left Manoah's side and knelt beside her, Karmela meeting her on Talia's other side. Together, the two of them held her, letting her weep. Other women from the city took up a similar wail, until the entire hillside rang with the echoes of their cries.

How long they knelt there, Raya could not tell except for the numbness creeping into her legs. She glanced at Karmela and together they managed to coax Talia to stand. Chaim came close and Talia fell into her son's arms. Raya returned to Manoah's side, and silence fell as the somber group made their way back to the city.

Weeks passed and Manoah slowly improved until the day came when Raya breathed with relief that he was no longer in danger of infection. And yet with all of the searching the servants had done, no one seemed to be able to find Samson to tell him of the damage the Philistines had committed against his family.

Raya stood at the door to the house and watched the road, hoping beyond hope that she might find him coming around the next bend to surprise them as he had done over a month ago. But watching the road and praying did nothing but cause her hope to wane.

She moved back into the house and sought Manoah. "You are going back out to work with the sheep?" He was ready, but she was not sure he was as strong as he could be. The injury had taken a toll, his limp more pronounced.

"Ariel cannot handle it alone, and the younger men are working the fields. I am ready." He put on his coat even as he leaned on the walking stick. "Do not worry about me, Raya. If I stay in this bed any longer, I will grow worse from boredom!"

She smiled. "I know." She kissed his cheek. "I will bring you food this afternoon. Where will you pasture today?"

"In the east pasture, farthest from Philistine territory." His look held determination, but she wondered if he was showing strength for her sake.

"I'll look for you there." She helped him to the door and watched him walk to the sheep pen, where Ariel met him. At least he still had one brother to work with. She took some comfort from that thought.

When he disappeared from sight, Raya turned to her room and knelt beside the couch, her head in her hands.

"Adonai, I do not know why I suffer so over the son You gave me. I do not know why You gave us a son only to have him run after the Philistines and disobey the very laws You wanted him to keep. Would it not have been better to give us a normal son who might stay and help his father and raise children for us to hold on our knees?" Tears fell onto the cushions. She hadn't realized until this moment how much she wished that Samson had been like her nephews, not chosen to be special in God's eyes. Being chosen seemed to only cause them all heartache.

"Forgive me, Lord. I do not deserve to question Your ways, but might You be willing to send Samson home one more time so we can tell him all that has happened? So I might hold him close once again?"

One visit would never be enough, she knew. But one more visit would appease her stricken heart for a time. And she was willing to ask for one rather than ask for nothing at all.

Samson wandered the hills along the Valley of Sorek, avoiding Delilah's house. He watched her from a distance, coming and going to visit her neighbors or even traveling farther to the markets in nearby Ekron. He searched her house on days when he knew she would not soon return but found nothing to prove his suspicions that she had been paid to turn him over to the Philistines. Perhaps they were waiting to pay her after she had come through on her promise.

Had she promised?

He stormed out of the house and again roamed the hills, frustrated that he cared for her at all. That he actually loved her mocked him. Did he love her? To what end? What did love even mean?

He lifted his gaze to the heavens, but God had remained silent to his doubts and desperate angst. The answers he sought remained elusive, and he could not satisfy his confusion.

A sudden desire to return home again surfaced. It had been over a month since he'd sat in judgment at Beth-Shemesh, where people in his family could find him. He did not know how his parents fared. They were not young as his aunts and uncles were in comparison.

He whirled about and took the road that led to Zorah. He would at least check on them. Perhaps he would even ask his father for advice. Then he would return to Delilah if he dared. And this time he would put an end to her questions once and for all.

Raya stood in the door, again looking at the road, a daily habit she had begun since Elead's death. The sun had barely risen and most of the household still slept, but she squinted to see what she longed for in the rising glow of dawn.

Thank You, Adonai, for the day when my faith will be seen and I will hold my son in my arms again. Thank You for whatever grace You might be willing to grant me this day as I continue to stand and wait…and hope.

Peace settled over her as she focused on praise to Adonai instead of simply crying out to Him. He was with her in some indefinable way, and He was equally with Samson, whether she could see it or not. Somehow God would make a way. She just wished she knew when and often wondered if she would live to see it.

She shaded her eyes as the sun rose, its rays pouring over the land and the road that led to Beth-Shemesh. And then she saw him, lumbering toward home, his bearing weighted and slow. Was it truly Samson? But she would know him anywhere, and she ran barefoot through the courtyard and down the path until she was in his arms again, weeping.

"You came! Oh how I prayed you would come!" She spoke into his chest, for he towered over her, but she didn't care that he nearly crushed her against him. How she had missed him!

He held her at arm's length. Searched her face. "Has something happened, Imma?" He looked haggard and she hated to tell him the truth, but he must know.

She nodded. "Yes. We tried to find you. Sent Chaim and then servants, but no one knew where you had gone."

"So you prayed. As you always do." He seemed different as he said it, as though he wasn't sure he believed her prayers had made any difference.

"Yes. I pray for you always, Samson. Your very birth was in answer to prayer." She met his gaze and saw skepticism in his eyes. What had become of him in the month he'd been away? Had Delilah caused this?

"What happened?" he asked again, as though the subject of praying was over.

"The Philistines came too close to the pastures where your father and Uncle Elead keep the sheep. They shot at your father and uncle with arrows." She paused, trying to read his expression, which had hardened. "Uncle Elead died from his wounds. Your father recovered and is back to helping Ariel with the sheep."

Samson braced himself with one hand against a tree. "How long ago?"

"Several weeks or more. We tried to find you, my son." She took his other hand and held it, afraid if she let go he might flee.

But he straightened and began to walk with her toward the house. "I will talk to my father. I want to hear all that happened from him too." He rested one arm about her shoulders and she leaned against him, grateful for his strength. One look at him told her that he had not broken the part of his vow involving his hair. But the hardness in his eyes made her wonder if he still believed in his purpose or the God who gave it to him.

"I'm glad you have finally come," she said, avoiding asking such questions. "I'm glad your father has lived to see you again."

He merely nodded and walked with her to the house.

CHAPTER TWENTY-THREE

Samson stayed with his parents a week, gathering all the details he could about the Philistines who had attacked his father and uncle, and made sure his father was truly well enough for him to leave.

Parting was harder than he had expected, and grief and anger filled him as he walked toward Delilah's house. He would pay back the Philistines for what they had done, of that he had no doubt. Just how to do so he wasn't sure.

He reached her house midday of a day's journey from Zorah and entered without knocking. She was in the gardens behind the house and greeted him with less than her usual warmth.

"You're back. I didn't think I would see you again." She pulled an onion from the earth and brushed the dirt from it.

"I don't intend to stay long." He wasn't sure he meant that, but he said it to irritate her.

"Then why come at all? Every time I ask you the secret of your strength, you leave me. How can I continue to live like this? You lie to me time after time, and then you walk away. What kind of a relationship is that?" She glared at him, minus her usual pout.

"You want to know the secret of my strength? Fine! I will tell you. But it will be the last time you ask. Then, you will help me to defeat these men of your people who put you up to this." He held her gaze until she looked away.

"What men? I don't know what you are talking about." But she would not look at him.

"Of course you do. Do you think me so foolish? You delude yourself." He turned on his heel and walked into the house. She followed, tossing the vegetables onto a wooden board before sitting beside him.

"Where have you been all this time?" Was she trying to make him think she cared? No. She cared nothing for him. But he would tell her about his hair and she could cut what she wanted and he would still defeat her people. And if he couldn't, he would die trying.

"I went home. Your people wounded my father and uncle. My uncle is dead because of them."

She looked stricken and brushed the hair from her eyes, then took his hand in hers. "I am sorry. I did not know."

"I'm surprised they did not tell you." He heard the scorn in his tone, but he wanted her to feel the full effect of his rage.

"Why would they tell me such a thing? You think I know more than I do, Samson." She leaned closer until he caught the scent of her perfume.

"You know more than you are telling me. Of that I am certain."

"And you do not tell me enough!" Her jaw tightened and she crossed her arms over her chest.

"And I am sick to death of your nagging, always asking me the same thing!" He released a pent-up breath. "We could have had a life, Delilah. But you wear a man down until he doesn't want you anymore."

She looked away, his words striking a greater blow than he intended. "Fine. I will not ask you anymore." She stood and walked to the cooking area.

He sat watching her, suddenly conscience-stricken. He'd been harsher than he intended, and somehow he couldn't bear to see her hurting.

He rose from the couch and stood opposite her. "My hair has never been cut," he said, "for I was dedicated to God as a Nazirite from birth. If my head were shaved, my strength would leave me, and I would become as weak as anyone else."

She looked at him. "You speak the truth this time."

He nodded. "And now I am in your power and as vulnerable as any man. You have knowledge you can use to destroy me, or you can prove your love for me and show me that you can keep this knowledge to yourself. Which will it be, Delilah?"

She looked down at the vegetables she'd begun to chop and did not answer for too long.

"I see," he said, defeat settling over him. She would betray him. He should leave now and not return. With the knowledge she bore, he was only one step away from a Philistine capturing him in his sleep and shaving his head. But better Delilah than someone else. Though he questioned his sanity with that reasoning.

He walked out the door and into the daylight, lifting his gaze heavenward. *Did I do the right thing? Will I capture the Philistines or will they capture me?*

But no answer came to him in that moment of uncertainty. The sun glinted off the hills like splayed fingers in the distance. He wasn't sure keeping his hair a secret was something that even mattered to God. But now that he'd told her, he was certain he would find out. One way or the other.

Raya felt the warmth of the sun spill over her face. She opened her eyes, startled and confused that she had slept so late. Manoah had apparently decided not to wake her as he had already left her side. She closed her eyes again, feeling a strange sensation move through her. She attempted to push herself into a sitting position and found her arms would not work as usual, a feeling of numbness overtaking them. The effort to rise caused her to break out in a sweat. Her breath came fast and her heart beat hard.

She moved her toes, but her legs also felt numb and tingly. She realized she would not be able to stand without help. What had happened to her? She had gone to sleep feeling fine. Had she been stricken with something in the night?

She attempted to call out, though her voice felt weak and thin like broth strained through thick cloth.

"Karmela! Talia! Someone help me!" She leaned against the wall, spent, certain that no one had heard her, surprised when the door opened.

"Raya! What is it?" Talia knelt at her side.

"My arms and legs are numb." And in that moment her head began to pound. She winced.

"How bad does it hurt?" Talia asked, obviously noticing her sudden pain. She touched Raya's arm. "Can you feel my touch?"

Raya blinked in an attempt to nod her head. "I have no strength." Tears filled her eyes. "What is happening to me, Talia?"

Talia shook her head. "I do not know. Let me get Karmela." She jumped up and left the room, quickly returning with Karmela.

"You slept later than usual," Karmela said. "Manoah told us to let you sleep—that you had been restless during the night. Do you remember that?"

Raya closed her eyes, thinking. "I dreamed of Samson, and though I can't remember the dream, it frightened me. I think I was restless out of fear. But how would that make me weak now?"

"I've heard of this," Karmela said. "It is called apoplexy. If that is what this is." Karmela felt Raya's head. "You have no fever."

Raya's mind spun, but the images she saw made no sense and her eyes were too heavy to keep open.

"What should we do?" Talia asked Karmela, her voice low. "How do we help her?"

Silence followed the remark. "I will mix some herbs," Karmela said at last. "Perhaps something will help."

"She appears to be in pain. Perhaps some white willow bark as well," Talia said.

Raya heard them move about the room, but she could not help them. Could not keep her mind focused on what they were doing. *Adonai?* But no prayers would come, nor did she know what to ask of Him.

Perhaps Samson would come and all would be well. But that made no sense. Samson could not fix her body, and something was definitely wrong with her body. Where was Manoah? But of course, the sheep needed him.

She forced her eyes to open, but the sun coming through the window made her head hurt more. Talia and Karmela would help her. Surely they would. She was too young to be bound to her bed or worse, die. She had too much yet to do and too many prayers to pray. Samson needed her prayers. She could sense it even amid the confusion of her thoughts. Why he needed her prayers, she did not know, but she attempted to intercede for him even in her pain.

Samson rested his head in Delilah's lap and allowed her to lull him into a state of complete relaxation. He wouldn't sleep, but she did have a way of removing all of his tension, which he continually found himself drawn to.

Darkness descended and it felt as though she still ran her fingers along his temples and through his hair. But how could she get her fingers through the braids? He thought to ask her, but the sensation of her touch was too inviting to risk having her stop.

Footsteps sounded distant, but surely it was part of the dream, until he heard her voice in his ear, first whispered softly then shouted, as though to make sure he heard her.

"Samson! The Philistines have come to capture you!"

He awoke slowly, still enchanted by the dream of her touch. Never mind that he had told her the truth about his strength. He would free himself as he had each time before.

He rose, opened his eyes to see five men standing around Delilah. Ropes held his hands tightly behind his back. He moved to snap them as he had before, but the ropes held. He tried again, writhing and attempting to stand, but his feet were also bound, and to his sudden dismay he looked at his captors and for the first time felt real fear.

Adonai! But as he turned his head and no longer felt the weight of the braids hanging from his head, the hair splayed over the floor at his feet, he knew God had left him. His strength had betrayed him, for the strength most certainly was in the length of his hair. Not in any other part of his vow which he had broken, but in the promise to never cut his hair.

"So you are truly as weak as any other man," one of the Philistine lords said to him, spitting in his face.

Samson looked at Delilah, who held a goatskin bag of coins in her hand, her expression carrying a slight smile. Defeat settled over him, and he told himself he was every bit a fool as ever there was one.

"Take your last look at her," said another of the men surrounding her. He walked toward Samson with a knife in his hand, and Samson braced himself to die.

But the man did not kill him. He grabbed Samson's head and dug out both of his eyes. Pain shot through Samson's entire body, and his head pounded. Darkness fell like a living thing over the very place, the people he could hear taunting, jeering, laughing at him. Was that Delilah's laughter joining with the men?

Nausea came in waves as someone replaced the ropes with metal chains. Someone—more than one?—untied the bonds around his ankles and he felt the rough arms of two men lift him to his feet.

God in heaven, help me! But he knew. God was not coming to help him this time. He would receive no answer to prayer. Even his mother's prayers, if she still prayed them, were of no use to him now. God had left him.

An overwhelming desire to weep overtook him, but he pushed it down, anger rising to replace the emotion. He would not show his agony to these uncircumcised Philistines! With every forced step, he felt the rough ground beneath his sandals and the strong grip of the same two men digging into his forearms. Arms that once proudly defeated their fellow Philistines.

The walk took too many steps to count, the distance impossible to guess without his sight. Where were they taking him? But all he could feel was pain. And he would not ask.

At last he heard them speaking to someone—a guard perhaps. "We've captured Samson," one man said, his voice jubilant. The man turned, for his voice came closer now. "Welcome to Gaza's prison, Samson. You can grind grain like a woman the rest of your pitiful life. You who thought you would take us down. How far you have fallen."

They tossed him into a small space with a dirt floor and solid walls, and as their footsteps faded away, Samson could still hear their laughter. Darkness and sounds he could not quite make out surrounded him. What a fool he had been! But even the thought did not remove the pain that had grown stronger with each labored step to this forsaken place.

He would die here. How long until hunger and thirst or vermin overtook him? Didn't he deserve every bit of this for all his boasting and doubts and forgetting his God? This time he could not restrain the tears that somehow still slid down his face despite his missing eyes. He curled into himself on the dirt floor and gave into the emotion, not caring if the Philistines heard him. No one would care what happened to him here. Not even God.

He held on to one consolation, that his mother could not see him now.

CHAPTER TWENTY-FOUR

One month after Raya was stricken with immobility, she woke to a new dawn, suddenly able to walk unaided. She moved into the courtyard to take in the warmth of the sun, gratitude filling her.

"It is so good to see you well again, Raya," Talia said, coming to sit beside her. "But you must take it slow. Let us do the work while you enjoy our company."

Raya smiled, relieved to simply breathe outside air instead of that in her stuffy room.

"We will clean your linens and let the air cleanse your room while you sit with us," Karmela said, pointing to her two daughters-in-law and sending them to do the task.

"Manoah left some time ago, didn't he?" They'd been letting her sleep, so she could never be sure when he left, only when he returned.

"He and Ariel are keeping far from Philistine territory, pasturing again in the east. Chaim went in search of Samson again. We wanted to be sure you were going to live," Talia said, her expression wreathed in concern. "You scared us for a while, Raya."

"How long ago did he leave? Samson is no doubt still with Delilah." Though a part of her wondered. Why did she feel such unease in her spirit every time she thought of her son?

"Chaim's been gone three days." Talia's brows knit as though the admission troubled her. "He should be home soon."

Raya nodded. She had used her strength simply to walk to the courtyard, and she leaned against the bench to close her eyes. She was getting stronger, wasn't she? And yet a part of her did not know. Somewhere in her spirit she knew something was not right, yet she couldn't explain the feeling.

The women worked, chatting as they ground the grain and chopped the vegetables. In the distance, she could hear Karmela's daughters-in-law talking as they walked past them toward the spring where they would wash the linens of her bed. She should be doing the work for them. But she had little strength.

Did Samson feel this way too? All of a sudden she saw him, reaching for her but unable to draw close. She drew in a sharp breath. Samson could not come. And his strength no longer protected him.

"Raya, are you all right?" Karmela's concern caused Raya to open her eyes and meet her gaze.

Raya slowly nodded then changed her mind and shook her head. "Actually, no. I need to lie down again." But the linens were gone from her bed.

Talia stood and sat beside her. "Your face is nearly ashen. What troubles you, my sister?"

Raya gripped the side of the bench, the sun no longer warm, having slipped behind a cloud. "Something has happened to Samson." Her heart pounded with the knowing. "I don't know what it is, just that he is in trouble."

Talia and Karmela exchanged a look. Both came beside her and helped her to her feet. "You are still tired, Raya. Come inside and rest on the cushions in the sitting room while the girls wash your bedding. When Chaim returns, I'm sure you will find you are mistaken."

Raya was not mistaken. She knew it as well as she knew the date of Samson's birth. But she did not argue. She leaned on the strength of her sisters-in-law and allowed them to place her among the sitting room cushions. Talia opened a window to let the light in and they left the door open so she could hear them. More likely so they could hear her.

She sank down and closed her eyes again, tears rising to the surface. *Samson, my son, what have you done?*

Chaim returned two days later, taking longer than Talia had expected, and Raya forced herself to join the family as he entered the main room of the house just before sunset.

"My son." Talia held him close then allowed him to greet his wife and children. "What did you learn?" Talia had spoken before Manoah could.

Chaim settled onto one of the seats and accepted food from his wife then faced Manoah and Raya. "I could not find Samson. But the Philistines were not afraid to tell me that they had captured him. Apparently the story of Delilah's treachery has now spread wide. They say that he told her the secret of his strength, and she had a Philistine shave his head while she lulled him to sleep on her lap. The Philistines paid her well, and they dragged him off to prison in Gaza." He dipped his bread into the stew and ate, looking away from Manoah and Raya as if he didn't want any questions.

"In prison," Manoah said, his voice distant.

Raya stared at her nephew. He was withholding something, but she could not imagine what. Had the Philistines hurt him when they captured him? She felt as though a millstone had landed on her. What little strength she had evaporated with the news. She would never see her son again. She knew it now. Either he would die in prison or she would die of this strange malady before then, but she knew her prayers for him no longer mattered. What good could they do with him locked away, probably in chains?

"Take me to my room," she said to Manoah.

His look held concern, but he merely stood and helped her to her feet. What would she do without Manoah? Talia managed alone, but Talia was younger and strong. And though she was heartbroken over Elead's loss, she had her family to comfort her. Raya had only Manoah who truly understood. And even he could not fully grasp the connection Raya felt to this only child she had spent her life training and serving and loving.

Not even Samson understood a mother's love, which led to a mother's constant prayers. She lowered her body to the bed, sweat rising on her forehead, her strength spent.

"I will check on you soon," Manoah said. "And bring you something to eat. You hardly touched your food."

"I couldn't eat if I wanted to," she said, tears spilling over onto her cheeks. "I just need to rest."

And perhaps if she tried she could pray. Despite her denials, Samson would need her prayers, maybe more so now than he ever had. Prison would change him—either harden him or soften him, but if he lived, he would not be the same for his disobedience and this Philistine punishment. Would he come to his senses there and realize that God had been with him all along? That God truly had called him from birth? She knew he questioned and fought the calling he'd been given, had done so for a long time. What would it take to help him to see that she had been telling him the truth? He was a gift from God with a call on his life, chosen of God. Would prison teach him that fact?

Raya rolled with Talia's help onto her side and tried to chew the broth-soaked bread she was offered. But one bite was all her stomach could handle. "I'm sorry," she said, looking into Talia's worried face.

Talia knelt beside her. "It is all right, Raya. You are tired." She leaned back on her heels, assessing her. "I think you are weary of life."

Raya nodded. Hadn't she known it since the malady had come upon her? "What news have you heard?"

Manoah had sent servants to Gaza over the past several months, always in search of more information. He tried to hide it, but she could tell that her husband was as troubled about Samson as she was.

But Manoah was stronger now, and he had taken charge of the household as never before. The clan had always looked to him as the oldest son, but Elead had been his right hand. Without Elead, he relied on Ariel, who supported him completely. Raya silently thanked God that Elead's death had not sown discord in the family. So Manoah could lead them in what to do and seemed to spend even less time with her except to check on her in her weakness.

"Samson still lives," Talia said. "One of the servants was able to see him after bribing a guard."

"He didn't tell Samson about me, did he? I don't want him to worry." She still needed to pray for him, but she wouldn't have him concerned that she lay dying while he could do nothing to help her.

Was she dying? She often wondered, but then her strength would renew and she thought she might grow well again, as Manoah had done after he was wounded.

"He told Samson nothing to upset him. But I fear he brought back news that might upset you." Talia stopped.

Raya forced herself to sit up. "Does Manoah know this upsetting news? Did Chaim know it from the beginning? I always sensed he was holding something back from me."

Talia touched Raya's arms in a comforting gesture. "You must not be angry with Chaim. We have all been so worried about you."

"Tell me what you know." Of course they would worry. She worried more than she should, but she was not afraid to meet the God who made her. She had met His angel. She knew that to meet Him would be glorious. She only wished she could first see her son again.

"They gouged out Samson's eyes. He can no longer see, Raya."

The words hit Raya like a blow and she swayed, held securely in Talia's arms. No eyes? "They arc barbarians!" She had heard of the cruelties of war, but Samson was not so big a threat that they needed to blind him.

"If only I could go to him." Raya drew in a breath and slowly released it. "But only my prayers can reach him. Do you think they reach him? Do you think God hears?" She had never confided her doubts to anyone but God.

Talia took Raya's hand and held it. "I believe God hears our prayers. Whether they reach Samson is up to God. But you are right to pray for him. We all pray for him. It is the only thing we have, and we have to cling to what we know is true. Moses taught us to pray, and we must listen to him."

Raya felt the slightest sense of relief. Talia always knew the right words to say to help her in times of need. But as she thought of Samson's loss of sight, her heartbeat slowed and weariness overtook her again. As though she was tied to the life of her son, she felt the pain of his loss. And she seemed unable to stop the grief.

Samson's life now consisted of turning the millstone, grinding the grain given to him each day. They fed him little but enough to give him the strength to work, and as the months passed, he felt his hair growing. First to his ears, then to his shoulders. And with the weight of his hair, he sensed his strength slowly returning.

Alone in his cell, he wept in silence. Every time he touched his face, he felt nothing beneath the closed lids. Anger flared when he thought of what they had done to him, but as he lay down on the ground to rest, he realized he had done this to himself. And with that thought, he lifted his gaze to the heavens, though they were no longer visible to him.

"I should have trusted You, Adonai. I should have obeyed You and lived the life You gave me without fighting every law along the way. I blamed Imma instead of believing her." Grief filled him. How hard his actions must have been on her.

I am sorry, he prayed silently. *I have failed You. Have mercy on me, Adonai. Forgive the sins of Your servant.*

He continued his silent plea, but as he did so, a sense of calm and peace came over him. *The strength never came from my hair.* His strength was a gift from God alone. And he had wasted the gift.

He rolled over and knelt, though he did so with some struggle on the hard stone floor. The Philistines did nothing to make prison pleasant for their captives and he suspected that they took great delight in having captured him.

Give me another chance, Adonai, my God. Let me obey You one more time and take the Philistines to Sheol with me. Another chance would surely mean his own death, for he could not see to attack anyone. But he knew with all of his heart that he wanted that chance. Wanted it more than he wanted his next breath. *Let my last breath count for You.*

He closed the lids that once covered his eyes and continued to pray long into the night. So this was why Imma prayed so often. God felt nearer to him now than at any other time in his life. He only wished he had not waited so long to make such an enormous and life-giving discovery.

PART SIX

Then Samson prayed to the Lord, "Sovereign Lord, remember me again. O God, please strengthen me just one more time. With one blow let me pay back the Philistines for the loss of my two eyes." Then Samson put his hands on the two center pillars that held up the temple. Pushing against them with both hands, he prayed, "Let me die with the Philistines." And the temple crashed down on the Philistine rulers and all the people. So he killed more people when he died than he had during his entire lifetime.

—Judges 16:28–30 (NLT)

CHAPTER TWENTY-FIVE

I'm going to try to see Samson," Manoah told Raya a month later. She had grown slightly stronger, but she knew in her spirit that her life would never be what it had been. The song that once filled her with joy in Adonai's presence or during the years she had raised her son seemed impossible to find again, though she did not let that stop her from thanking God for His kindness to her.

Raya stood beside Manoah and placed a hand on his chest. "It is a long walk to Gaza, my husband. What if the Philistines recognize you and capture you as well? They already shot you once. Have you forgotten they killed your brother?"

"I will not dress as the head of my tribe. Chaim will accompany me as well as a number of servants. If I can't see him, I at least want to find out if he still lives." Manoah wrapped the turban about his head and took his staff in hand. "Ariel will handle things while we are gone. Please do not fear, Raya. I promise to be careful."

Raya studied his face, reminding herself that he had always been a godly, careful man. "I will pray that you return safely." She kissed his cheek and smiled, not wanting him to fear for her. It was clear that his decision was made and to argue with him would only cause strife.

She walked with him to the door where Chaim and the servants waited. He looked at her once more then waved as he left. She stood at the door, watching until she could no longer see them.

"They will be all right," Talia said, joining her. "Chaim always returns safely."

"Chaim hasn't tried to see Samson," Raya said, still watching the road. "The Philistines are emboldened now that they have Samson." She looked at Talia. "If they could shoot our husbands before they captured Samson, what makes our men think they won't do worse to them now that Samson is no longer able to protect them?" She had wanted to say the words to Manoah, but he wouldn't have listened. She feared that he was growing reckless as he aged instead of wiser. He would never have suggested such a thing as to enter Gaza in years past.

Talia did not respond to Raya's outburst, and for the first time Raya realized that her sister-in-law was as worried as she was. Her normally cheerful spirit had disappeared with the sorrow in her gaze. "You are right," Talia said at last. "We should have stopped them."

"They would not have listened." The thought to send someone after them even now entered Raya's mind, but she knew Manoah would dismiss her concerns. He wanted to see his boy or at least attempt to find out how he fared. Had the Philistines already killed him? But her spirit did not think so.

"Well, there is nothing to be done about it now but wait," Talia said, her tone sounding slightly defeated. But a moment later she rallied. "It will be well. You'll see. In the meantime, perhaps you can help me with the lentils."

She could do that much. "I can sort lentils," she said, though her heart still carried a weight of concern. *Please, Adonai, don't let me lose Manoah too.*

Samson turned the grindstone with rhythmic sameness. Voices sounded in the distance, coming closer, and he listened, aware that his sense of hearing was better than it had been.

Laughter drifted on the stale air as some of the guards passed by. "They say the festival is going to be the biggest one they've ever given to praise Dagon," one of the guards said.

"And all because of Dagon's help in capturing Samson." The second guard nearly shouted the words, certainly for Samson's benefit. More laughter followed, trailing off into the distance.

Oh, Adonai, I am sorry to have brought this disgrace on Your name. If only he had embraced the call and listened to the teaching of his parents. He'd wanted everything they told him he couldn't have. Somehow being told he couldn't had caused him to want it more. What a fool he'd been.

He turned the stone, listening to the grating noise, wondering if he would hear human voices again today, certain he wouldn't. They didn't even speak to him when they brought what they called food. He would have eaten the grain he was grinding if they didn't weigh every bit of it to make sure he didn't do just that.

His stomach growled in protest. He'd lost weight. He could tell when he felt his body. They were keeping him weak. For what reason? It wasn't like he could find his way out of prison and hurt them now.

But they had already hurt him enough. And his constant prayer always ended with him destroying the Philistines, even if he had to die with them.

Three days later, Raya took up the shuttle and attempted to weave a small garment for one of her great-nephews. Talia sat opposite her, helping. "I'm glad you are feeling strong enough to do more things," she said, handing Raya a red thread to weave through the others attached to the loom.

"I have to do more than sleep or sit and worry." She worked the shuttle to deftly weave the thread through the warp.

"Well, it is good to see you up and about again." Talia smiled.

"The men should be heading back soon," Raya said, changing the subject.

"I would think so. If they even entered Gaza, the walk is not so far. If they hurried, they could make the trip in less than a week." Talia took a turn with the shuttle and wove in the next strand. They continued to work in harmony with Talia quietly humming.

Raya felt her spirits lift. Music had such a calming effect on her. Why had she allowed herself to lose her song? Why had she allowed duty and worry to burden her and prayer to become requests of God more than praise for what He had already done?

The thoughts left her feeling slightly chastened. She would find her song again. She joined in with Talia, creating harmony to Talia's higher notes, to show herself she could be happy despite her circumstances.

But a moment later the door burst open, silencing both of them.

Karmela's expression could not hide her concern. "They've returned."

Raya and Talia jumped up at the same time and followed Karmela into the courtyard. Raya searched the group for Manoah. The servants blocked her view of the donkey Manoah had ridden.

Chaim stepped forward. He grasped Raya's arms. "Aunt Raya." He simply held her then, saying nothing more.

"Manoah?" She tried to push past Chaim, but he held her fast. She fought against him. "Where is Manoah?" He finally released her and she hurried to the donkey's side. A body lay draped over its bulging sides.

"Manoah!" She fell to her knees, screaming his name. Then a wild keening sound came from her lips, for she could not silence her pain.

Talia and Karmela came toward her and held her close, but the rest of the day blurred before her. Chaim and Amichai, Ariel, and his sons quickly built a bier before the sun set and they half carried Raya to the tomb where Manoah's brother already lay.

No explanation yet of what had happened. Bandits. She'd heard that word, but silence had been the only sound to interrupt the weeping. Raya would not be put off to help in washing his body, his wounds. Taking his face in her hands one last time.

Her mind could not even think to pray, for surely God had abandoned her. She had prayed for his safety, but safety had not kept him. And God was not listening.

Ariel attempted to say kind words about Manoah, and the men quickly rolled the stone away and carried him inside. Before she had time to let the truth sink into her heart, her husband lay in a stone cave wrapped in grave clothes.

This could not be her life. She was not strong like Talia. She had told Manoah she could not live without him. Why had he tried to see Samson and get so close to Philistine territory?

The questions tormented her as the others led her on shaky legs toward home. She prayed, as she laid her head on the bed Manoah should be sharing, that she would not wake up again.

Samson awoke to a hand on his arm, shaking him. "Get up! Today is your day!" The guard laughed, and then a second guard took his other arm. Together they led him to a cold bath, gave him hyssop, and told him to wash. Did they want him clean so he looked good when they killed him?

He shivered in the bath, but the hyssop worked heat into his skin. He scrubbed months of grime from his body, hoping he hadn't missed a spot.

"Time's up," one of the guards said. They pulled Samson from the bath and threw clothes at him. "I assume you can still figure out how to dress yourself."

The other laughed. "We might have to help him. They want him looking good, remember?"

Samson felt his cheeks heat. That these men should see him naked and then have to dress him when he couldn't see what they were doing was the ultimate humiliation. But he held his tongue and submitted to their "help."

"There, he looks good enough," one said. They grabbed his arms again and guided him outside. He could tell they were in the open air, for he felt the warmth of the sun on his cheeks. He breathed deeply, lifting his head a moment and whispering a silent thanks to Adonai. Something was changing in him as they walked him first across stones then a dirt road. His strength was returning. His God had heard his prayers.

He sensed that he could easily knock these two guards to the dust, but he kept himself pretending weakness. Two Philistines was not what he had in mind.

And then he heard them in the distance. "Our god has given us victory over our enemy Samson!"

"Hurry up," the guard to his left said. "They've already begun the sacrifices."

Samson kept their pace, though he still feigned weakness.

The sound of a large crowd shouting and reveling met his astute ears. The guards stopped close enough to them so apparently the people could see him.

"Our god has delivered our enemy to us! The one who killed so many of us is now in our power!" Samson heard the taunts and sarcastic tone in many of the voices.

After the guards paraded him around a small area, they moved him out of sight and tied his arms to a tree branch. Samson considered snapping the rope, but the time was still not right.

Raya could not sleep but neither could she move, and for a moment she wondered if another bout of apoplexy had hit her. She had never in her life struggled to pray. Since she had first learned to repeat the prayers of her mother, she had spoken to God about all that was on her heart. Even when she had accepted that she would not be a mother, she had still prayed and thanked Him for Manoah and his family.

Now she could not even groan as Talia had done when Elead had passed. Wasn't this the way of all the earth? A person was born, lived a few years, then was gathered to his or her fathers and mothers who had normally gone before them.

She closed her eyes. She was glad Samson had not been here to see his father at the last. Her son could die soon. Who knew how long the Philistines would let him live? God had allowed them both to be taken from her.

The thought brought such pain that her head seemed to explode. She tried to rise from the pallet, but the weight of the pain bore down on her. She should call Talia, Karmela, somebody. She closed her eyes instead and thought she beheld the face of the angel she'd seen that long ago day.

Samson remained in the shadow, listening to the crowd growing wilder. Slurred speech came from somewhere above him. He lifted his head at the sound of his name.

"Bring out Samson so he can amuse us!" The shouts grew to a chant until a servant, or perhaps it was a guard, untied the ropes, took his hand, and led him into the temple again.

Samson felt as much as heard the venom in their taunts, their mocking tone. The servant leaned close to be heard above the noise.

"Are you able to stand here?" The voice sounded like that of a young boy, and he seemed uncertain as to whether he had put Samson in the right spot.

Samson lifted his head and felt spittle hit his face. The crowd was obviously on the roof of the temple. *Please, Adonai.* But he had already pleaded for mercy. The rest was up to God whether to truly restore his strength.

At last he answered the boy. "Place my hands against the pillars that hold up the temple. I want to rest against them."

"There are a lot of people above you, even the lords of the Philistines," the boy said. "Thousands of people are watching you, so don't do anything foolish." He seemed nervous, but what had he to fear from a blind man, unless God had put that fear in his heart?

"I won't," he promised the boy, but as he felt the young man's presence move away from him and heard the noise of the crowd growing ever louder and more obscene and taunting, he lifted his face again to the sky and quietly prayed, "Sovereign Lord, remember me again. O God, please strengthen me just one more time. With one blow let me pay back the Philistines for the loss of my two eyes."

He braced himself squarely between the two center pillars and drew in a deep breath. It was now or not at all.

Voices startled Raya, and she heard Talia, Karmela, and the other members of her family gathering around her. She tried to open her eyes, but they wouldn't lift. She heard them, could feel them, but she could not make out their words. She turned her thoughts to Samson, sensing in that moment that he needed her prayers now more than ever.

Be with him, Adonai. Whatever it is he needs from You, please grant it.

She saw the angel hovering in the distance and the voices growing dimmer, but then she saw Samson in her mind's eye surrounded by Philistines.

Whatever he needs, Lord. Please help him.

She tried to see what it was he needed, but only the brightness of the angel filled her vision.

Samson braced himself on the two pillars holding the temple, the strongest part of the temple roof. Without them the roof would collapse. He would be crushed beneath the weight as surely as the Philistines standing above would fall to their deaths.

He did not care. This was the moment he had prayed for, and he hoped God would have mercy on him one more time and let him end his life better than he had lived it.

Bracing hard against the pillars, he felt the anointing strength of old fill him. He pushed with all his might and cried, "Let me die with the Philistines!"

He heard the roar of boulders crashing, felt the pillars give way under his strength, heard the screams of the people, until the roof fell, and all went silent.

Raya felt a sense of deep peace move through her like water flowing gently over rocks. She lifted a hand toward the angel of the Lord, and in that moment, as she took his hand, she saw Samson's smiling face behind him.

In the distance Manoah stood, as if they were both beckoning her, but it was the glory of the angel of the Lord she longed for. She had long wanted to see him again, and now he took her hand and pulled her into his warm embrace.

She was finally home, all of her prayers answered.

AFTERWORD

Later his brothers and other relatives went down to get his body. They took him back home and buried him between Zorah and Eshtaol, where his father, Manoah, was buried. Samson had judged Israel for twenty years.

 —Judges 16:31 (NLT)

AUTHOR'S NOTE

As I wrote the story of Samson's mother, whom I gave the name Raya, which means "beloved wife; friend," I came upon several challenges. One was how to tell this story from Raya's point of view when so much of scripture is all about Samson. I found I had to add Samson's point of view as well to give depth to Raya's feelings and a better understanding of her character.

Second, as I wrote this story, I found myself surprised at how Samson was chosen of God from before his birth, set apart to do God's will, and yet God allowed Samson to make his own choices, which eventually led to his downfall. How like us he was! But in the end, God got through to his heart, and Samson recognized his own folly and returned in faith to the God who had made him. I find joy in that knowledge because it gives hope to all of us in our human condition. All of us have to choose whether or not we will follow the Lord and do the things He created us to do. How loving is our God that He gave us the ability to choose and yet at the same time He chooses us to be His own! It is a paradox we will never fully understand on this earth.

Lastly, I found that at the end of the Judges account of Samson's life, scripture says that his "brothers" came to get his

241

body to bury him in the cave of his father Manoah. But nowhere else in the narrative are brothers of Samson mentioned. So I looked through my Greek/Hebrew study Bible for answers and discovered that "brothers" can be used as meaning direct siblings having the same parents or it can also refer to cousins or relatives in a more general sense. It was unclear in this case as to which interpretation to take, so I decided to have his "brothers" actually be his cousins, which could have been true.

I hope you enjoyed my take on the story of Samson's unnamed mother. Raya is the name I gave her, but only God knows her real name, as is true of many women in scripture. But whether God reveals their names to us or not, we know this woman existed, that she saw the angel of the Lord and spoke with him, that he promised her a child, and that she obeyed God's commands in raising Samson as a Nazirite. The rest— how she felt about her life and the people in her family, and how Samson's life affected hers—is from my imagination. As a mother of sons, I can attest that a mother never forgets her child and a woman of faith prays for her children continually no matter how old they are.

A mother's strength, Raya's source of strength, came from her trust in the Lord. She grew in that strength and faith as she walked with Him and called on Him in prayer. May each of us learn to do the same.

In His grace,
Jill Eileen Smith

FACTS BEHIND the *Fiction*

✦

THE SHOFAR

When people in Samson's day wanted to make noise—whether in war or worship—they blew into the ancient version of a bugle: the curved and sometimes curled horn of a male goat.

The ram's horn (*shofar* in Hebrew) sounds like a bugle and is loud enough that people called the musician playing it the Blast Master. Bible writers mention this horn more than any other musical instrument.

The Bible's most famous story involving rams' horns took place outside the city walls of Jericho a century or more before Samson.

"When you hear the priests give one long blast on the rams' horns, have all the people shout as loud as they can. Then the walls of the town will collapse" (Joshua 6:5 NLT).

The horn couldn't hit more than a few pitches, each determined by the position of the Blast Master's lips—what brass players call the *embouchure* (ahm-boo-shur). But it didn't take many notes to call Jews to worship or to launch a battlefield attack. Different patterns could send different messages. One long note could tell soldiers to attack. Staccato bursts could call a retreat.

In times of high anxiety, the loud blast could terrify people—as it did the day God came down to Mount Sinai to address the people Moses led during the Exodus.

"On the morning of the third day, thunder roared and lightning flashed, and a dense cloud came down on the mountain. There was a long, loud blast from a ram's horn, and all the people trembled" (Exodus 19:16 NLT).

Rams' horns come in different sizes and shapes. They are naturally hollow, but horn makers cut a small hole at the pointed tip of the horn. The Blast Master blows into the hole to produce the sound.

Jews today blow the horn in the synagogue on special occasions, such as at the end of Yom Kippur. Yom Kippur is the national day of repentance, which is the holiest day of the year for Jewish people.

NAZIRITES, PROMISED TO GOD

When people of faith today want to express their love to God in a deeper way or perhaps for a special occasion, they fast. For a stretch of time, they abstain from something, usually by limiting their food intake.

People in Bible times fasted too. But they also had the option of devoting themselves to God by taking a Nazirite vow—for a limited time or for life.

Moses outlined the guidelines for this vow. Forbidden while under a Nazirite vow:

- Beer
- Wine
- Vinegar
- Grapes or raisins
- Haircuts. "Even the hair of a Nazirite is sacred to me...you must never cut your hair" (Numbers 6:5 CEV).
- Dead people. "Never go close to a dead body, not even that of your father, mother, brother, or sister" (Numbers 6:6-7 CEV).

NAZARITES WERE FORBIDDEN TO PARTAKE IN, OR EVEN TOUCH, RAISINS OR GRAPES OR ANYTHING MADE WITH THEM.

If someone died suddenly near a Nazirite man, the Nazirite had to shave his head, offer animal sacrifices for ritual cleansing, and then start the vow over.

Jewish Christians apparently also took the Nazirite vow (Acts 21:23–24). Many Bible experts speculate that Paul took a Nazirite vow for a short time: "He had his head shaved...because he had made a promise to God" (Acts 18:18 CEV).

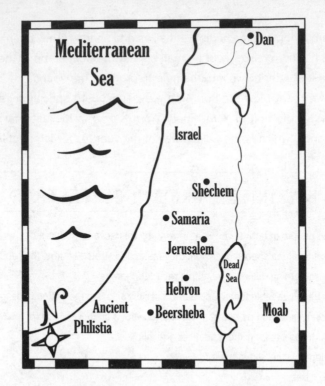

ANCIENT PHILISTIA TO THE WEST AND ISRAEL TO THE EAST. THE PHRASE "FROM DAN TO BEERSHEBA" APPEARS NINE TIMES IN THE BIBLE TO MEAN THE ENTIRE PEOPLE—ALL TWELVE TRIBES—OF ISRAEL.

PHILISTINES IN THE PROMISED LAND

Armed with bronze weapons, Joshua and the Exodus Hebrews crossed the Jordan River and stormed into what are now Palestinian Territories and Israel.

The Philistines were already there, armed with iron weapons and iron-armored chariots. They had settled into five main cities along the southern coast and the Judean foothills: Gaza, Ashkelon, Ashdod, Gath, and Ekron.

Joshua's forces could not conquer them. So the southland Israelites avoided the Philistines and settled in Judean hills, where chariots couldn't run over them like tanks over infantry.

The Philistines protected their secret for forging iron. "Whenever the Israelites wanted to get an iron point put on a cattle prod, they had to go to the Philistines. Even if they wanted to sharpen plow-blades, picks, axes, sickles, and pitchforks they still had to go to them. And the Philistines charged high prices" (1 Samuel 13:20-21 CEV).

It's a mystery where the Philistines came from. The most common guess is from somewhere in the Aegean Sea area, such as Greece or Crete, or islands in the region. DNA evidence from a large Philistine cemetery near Ashkelon seems to confirm that theory. The testing reveals a diverse gene pool at the time, with DNA drawing from a mix of locals and Europeans.

One wave of Philistines raided locations on the island of Cyprus, along with Turkey and Syria, before invading Egypt in about 1200 BC. Egyptians pushed them back and then engraved pictures of them as captives on the tomb walls of Rameses III (reigned 1186–1155 BC).

GOLIATH, THE PHILISTINE CHAMPION

A giant of a man—though Scripture calls him a champion, not a giant—Goliath stood about six feet, nine inches (2 meters) tall. Some translations of the Bible list his height at "six cubits and a span," or nine feet, 9 inches (1 Samuel 17:4 NIV), but older texts of the Bible, such as the Dead Sea Scrolls, say four cubits and a span, or six feet, nine inches. That puts him about a foot taller than the average man at the time, based on estimates from skeletons and mummies of the era.

Many scholars say the "giants" of the Bible were simply taller people who, today, might be considered good candidates to play basketball. The typical height of an NBA player is about six feet, seven inches (roughly 2 meters).

A PHILISTINE WARRIOR WITH HIS CHARACTERISTIC FEATHERED HELMET.

The Bible also reports the Israelites conquering the kingdom of "King Og of Bashan...the last survivor of the giant Rephaites" (Deuteronomy 3:11 NLT). Translators can't agree if the Israelites reported finding his "iron bed" or his "rock coffin." Whatever it was, the writer of Deuteronomy says it measured thirteen feet long and six feet wide (four by two meters). That would have been a comfy fit for the tallest man known so far, Robert Pershing Wadlow (1918–1940), at eight feet, 11 inches (2.7 meters).

AN ANCIENT EGYPTIAN RELIEF DEPICTS PHILISTINE CAPTIVES BEING LED AWAY AFTER THEIR FAILED INVASION OF EGYPT.

Goliath fell in mortal combat to a young man with a slingshot, in one of the most famous stories in the Bible (1 Samuel 17).

HOW THE ISRAELITES WORE THEIR HAIR

Long, dark, and well-kept is the way Israelite women seemed to prefer their hair. That was the style throughout much of the ancient Near East. Jews even wrote songs about hair: "Your hair is like a flock of goats streaming down Mount Gilead" (Song of Solomon 4:1 NCV).

Pictures from an Egyptian cemetery known as Beni Hassan showed hairstyles of traders from neighboring lands, such as Canaan and Israel. Women wore their hair down and over their shoulders. Men in the pictures look well-groomed with thick, short-cropped hair, which was nicely accessorized. They wore beards, which were neatly trimmed along the jawline, and no mustaches.

Women rarely cut their hair and often wore it plaited, or braided. Bible writers sometimes describe women modestly covering their hair with scarves or veils. Short hair was apparently common among most working-class men, perhaps because long hair took a lot of time, trouble, and money to maintain—as it does today. Men and women poured olive oil on their hair—sometimes scented. They used it as a conditioner, scalp moisturizer, and bug repellent.

WOODEN COMBS ABOUT 1360 BC.

A thousand years before anyone anointed the hair of Jesus with oil, musicians sang of such an expression of esteem. "You honor me by anointing my head with oil. My cup overflows with blessings" (Psalm 23:5 NLT).

The Law of Moses ordered Israelites not to shave back the hair on their forehead or at the sides. Scholars say this was apparently to counter a pagan tradition of cutting hair like that.

Samson wore seven braids to help manage his hair and keep it out of his way. Later, King David's son, Absalom, took pride in his thick, long hair. "He got his hair cut once a year, and when the hair was weighed, it came to about five pounds" (2 Samuel 14:26 CEV). He may have exaggerated a little, as crown

AN ANCIENT EGYPTIAN
POLISHED-SILVER MIRROR.

princes sometimes did, or he added a lot of olive oil. A year's growth of hair is typically about six inches, which would weigh a couple of ounces (about 60 grams).

Later, Absalom's long hairstyle was a direct cause of his untimely death—his hair snagged in a tree, and he was yanked off his mule during a battlefield retreat and left dangling as a bull's-eye for an enemy soldier (2 Samuel 18:14).

ANCIENT BENI HASSAN FRESCOS DEPICT HAIRSTYLES STYLES AND ATTIRE OF TRADERS FROM NEIGHBORING LANDS, SUCH AS WHAT IS NOW ISRAEL.

THE JUDGES WEREN'T REALLY JUDGES

Israel's dozen heroic leaders known as judges in the Old Testament Book of Judges didn't judge court cases—with one exception.

"Deborah would sit under the Palm Tree of Deborah, which was between the cities of Ramah and Bethel, in the mountains of Ephraim. And the people of Israel would come to her to settle their arguments" (Judges 4:5 NCV). But she's most famous for leading a volunteer army in Galilee that defeated an invading chariot corps, apparently with the help of a flash flood. "The Kishon River swept Sisera's men away" (Judges 5:21 NCV).

Similar leaders, such as Gideon, led Israelites when invaders or neighboring kingdoms raided them at harvest time, oppressed them with taxes, or tried to take them as slaves.

The dozen judges were all regional leaders. Israel didn't exist as a unified nation. The descendants of Abraham were still a loosely connected coalition of tribes, each tribe an extended family. The political arrangement was a bit like the United States, except without a federal government, with each state as its own tribe.

When an outsider threatened a tribe, the tribe defended itself, sometimes with the help of neighboring tribes. Jephthah led a coalition army to defeat Ammonites from what is now the country of Jordan (Judges 11). One tribe, Ephraim, sat out the war. Jephthah later retaliated, killing forty-two thousand people from Ephraim (Judges 12:6).

SAUL BRINGS THE ERA OF JUDGES TO AN END

Israel's first king, Saul, did little to unify the tribes during his reign of perhaps twenty-five years. He did create an army to protect what land the tribes had managed to take from Canaanites, which was still mostly in the central hill country. He and three of his sons died trying to stop an overwhelming force of Philistines.

It was King David in about 1000 BC who first transformed the tribes into the united nation of Israel. His son Solomon developed such a strong central government that it nearly erased the tribal system led by family elders. After Solomon's son Rehoboam inherited the throne and promised heavier taxes, the ten northern tribes started their own kingdom. That left Rehoboam king of his tribe of Judah and the tribe of Benjamin, which became the tiny southern Jewish nation, about the size of Puerto Rico or two Rhode Islands.

Fiction Author
JILL EILEEN SMITH

Jill Eileen Smith is the bestselling, award-winning author of the Wives of King David, Wives of the Patriarchs, and Daughters of the Promised Land series, as well as *The Heart of a King, Star of Persia*, and the nonfiction books *When Life Doesn't Match Your Dreams* and *She Walked Before Us*. Her research has taken her from the Bible to Israel, and she particularly enjoys learning how women lived in Old Testament times.

When she isn't writing, she loves to spend time with her family and friends, read stories that take her away, ride her bike to the park, snag date nights with her hubby, try out new restaurants, or play with her lovable, "helpful" cat, Tiger. Jill lives with her family in southeast Michigan.

Contact Jill through email (jill@jilleileensmith.com), her website (jilleileensmith.com), Facebook (facebook.com/jilleileensmith), or Twitter (twitter.com/JillEileenSmith).

Nonfiction Author
STEPHEN M. MILLER

Stephen M. Miller is an award-winning, bestselling Christian author of easy-reading books about the Bible and Christianity. His books have sold over 1.9 million copies and include *The Complete Guide to the Bible*, *Who's Who and Where's Where in the Bible*, and *How to Get Into the Bible*.

Miller lives in the suburbs of Kansas City with his wife, Linda, a registered nurse. They have two married children who live nearby.

Read on for a sneak peek of another exciting story
in the Ordinary Women of the Bible series!

MISSIONARY OF HOPE

by Ginger Garrett

ROME, 66 CE

Mamertine prison, the dungeon of Tullianum

Priscilla drifted between states of awareness. Sunlight did not exist here in the dungeon of Tullianum. The cold was a relentless adversary, never giving her a moment's peace. Every bone ached. Right now, her lower back ached as if someone were pressing burning rods to it. The nerves that had gone numb in her legs had only made a cruel, temporary bargain. When she shifted position to relieve her back, they would reawaken in fire.

Was it a dream that she could still smell the sea air and still feel the waves that carried her so far from this city? She had landed in Corinth on a bright day with brisk winds coming in from the ocean. She could taste the tang of brine that always hung in the air. Her hair had curled and frizzed the moment she stepped off the boat that day. She smiled at the memory, her dry lips cracking. That was the day she became a completely different woman, and she hadn't even known it.

And then Ephesus, oh Ephesus! She had imagined it to be a dark and terrible place, but the beauty of that city came back, even now. She closed her eyes, feeling the sunlight on her face. The beautiful mosaics, the limestone walls shimmering in the summer heat and the breeze that passed through evergreen branches. Yes, evergreen was the fragrance of Ephesus.

Wiping a tear from her eye, she felt her sharp cheekbones under a thick layer of grit and dirt. How long had she been here? She did not know. A guard told her that Aquila had been here too but had already "met his fate." She had been too weak to disagree. Aquila had met his Lord, and that was an altogether different thing.

Tullianum was rumored among the guards to be the gateway to the underworld. Long ago, the guards whispered, unfortunate men and women had been sacrificed in this spot during spring occult rituals. People always went to such desperate lengths to placate an invisible world. Why did they imagine that the invisible world was an angry one? If only she had the strength to tell them. Praise God the letters had been written. The word was in the world, and she had peace now as she left it.

Her mind turned to Aquila. Why could she not remember his fragrance? A tentmaker, he smelled of leather and sun and the rosemary sprigs he loved sprinkled over baked bread.

She closed her eyes again and dreamed of him. He was the rarest of men. Fully aware of his strength and power and yet so willing to see her grow into her own. He had bought his freedom from serving her family as their slave only to spend his life granting her freedom that no woman dared dream of. All because this God-man they followed, Jesus, had given them such radical new thoughts, a new vision for life, and a new covenant. But who among men had found the courage to act on Christ's words?

Aquila had. That was one reason why Priscilla had led a remarkable life. That was why, she knew, the tears fell as she dreamed. She was a woman who had been loved as no other woman had ever been loved before. Would there be others after her, she wondered? Would other women know such freedom? Would other women walk in both strength and love?

But one secret she must keep, she reminded herself. Even in sleep, she would not let herself dream of her son. She could never speak his name again, lest the guards pass this information on. No one was safe, no matter where they were. Even now, her son was on strange waters, his destination hidden from her.

She heard the guards whispering as she dreamed.

"Her hands move as she dreams!" a rough voice said.

"She is writing," another man answered. The two men laughed.

"Who are you writing, old woman?" the first voice asked. "No one is coming to save you."

Oh, but you are wrong. She smiled as she sank deeper into a feverish sleep.

Nineteen years earlier
ROME, 47 CE

The home smelled amazing. Priscilla peeked into the kitchen to watch the cooks at work. Thyme and rosemary had been chopped and prepared as a dry rub for the meat to be roasted. Onions and peppers were sliced and sat in bowls. A cook worked on barley and lentil soup. First, she sautéed spices over the fire to release their oils—dill, fennel, thyme—then added onion before putting them in the soup pot. Another cook tucked rosemary into every pot for a burst of fragrance and then into the bouquets of flowers as well.

Priscilla wondered if the meal would be wasted.

The desserts were lovely too, with dates soaked in honey, raisins, and pomegranates alongside a platter of roasted chestnuts drizzled with honey. She also spied tarts glazed with honey. Three servants worked feverishly in the kitchen, elbow to elbow.

Bowls of celery seed and bundles of dill sat unused on the table. Priscilla knew the herbs would be used for seasoning the flatbread. This was the bread used for sopping up the lamb's juices left in the bowl.

Maybe another bride would swoon with hunger. Were brides supposed to be hungry before their wedding? If only her mother were here to tell her what she should feel. Surely this cold dread settling in the pit of her stomach was not normal. Her mother would know how to chase it away.

She snuck back to her room and clutched her mother's wedding veil. The beaded linen had been recently bleached, but the family's crest embroidered in blue had lost none of its stark power against the white. Long ago, she had dreamed of the day she would wear this, but she never dreamed this day would come without her mother. What would Mother say about the man chosen as her husband?

"You did not attend the Trajan Forum yesterday."

"Father!" She jumped up. He stood at the door to her room.

He spoke in soft tones, all his strength lost since the death of her mother. He was a ghost of a man. Were the circles under his eyes darker? He so rarely slept. He cocked an eyebrow, waiting.

Priscilla exhaled, careful not to vent her frustration. "No, Father. I was hoping if you spent time alone with Marcellus, he would help you understand."

He cocked his head to one side, like a child. Her brother had obviously failed in the mission.

"There is still time to fix your mistake," she gently urged.

She stepped toward him then reached out and rested one hand on his arm. He recoiled, then seemed confused. Father was not himself anymore. Was this still grief from losing Mother? But that was two years ago. Was this old age? She feared that a disease was at work, but Marcellus laughed at the suggestion. Just as he had laughed when she insisted Father would never allow her to marry a former household servant. Even if that man was Aquila.

Yesterday, Aquila had officially become a citizen of Rome. Two years ago, before her death, Priscilla's mother had granted Aquila a letter of freedom, his manumission. She had written the letter, and Father had signed it. Yesterday, appearing before the Trajan Forum, Aquila had been officially listed in the census among the citizens of Rome.

Tomorrow he would become her husband. It was unthinkable. She was destined to marry someone in the courts of the emperor. Someone educated, wealthy, and influential. Someone like her. In the meantime, she was going to serve in the courts as a historian. She had already arranged it with her tutor. Emperor Claudius adored history, and no one was a better scholar than she.

Her father did not move. His eyes stared into the distance, so she spoke kindly and gently.

"This marriage makes no sense," she said. "Reverse it. You are a wealthy man. You are Athos, supplier of exotics for the emperor's games. You are the man who dares to cage lions and bears. All the earth is afraid of you, Father. Giving your daughter to a tentmaker? A freedman?"

Her father's eyes cleared as he turned to her. "I did no such thing."

She moved in closer, her words rushing together. In her haste, her voice rose in volume. "But you did! You allowed it! Father, tell Marcellus to cancel the wedding. I have a chance to serve in the emperor's courts. I will work with Emperor

Claudius, writing the history of Rome. You know how he loves history. This is how I will serve our family, and Rome. You've always wanted to leave a legacy to Rome! This is it, Father. This is how we'll do it. Now tell Marcellus—"

"Tell me what?"

Marcellus leaned against a pillar across from her room. Priscilla gasped. He was unpredictable lately—kind at times, vicious at others.

Her father looked between them both, his eyes glazing over again. Quickly, Marcellus closed the distance between them and took him by the arm.

"You've upset our father," Marcellus scolded her. "Are you really so selfish?" Turning to their father, he softened his countenance. "Come, Father, you need to lie down in your room." Lucian, the household steward, appeared and draped a shawl over her father's thin shoulders.

Marcellus and her father walked away, arm in arm, with Lucian following.

Priscilla said nothing. His words stung. She rubbed the veil between her fingers like it had something more to offer, something hidden beneath the beading and embroidery. Catching herself before she ruined it, she wondered why there was no escape from this misfortune. Her life had seemed so blessed just a few years earlier, her future secure.

Born and raised a Jew, she was one of God's chosen people, and the religious festivals marked each season with gladness. In recent years, some in her synagogue had begun embracing a version of their faith that included a risen Messiah named Jesus. They held that a second covenant was given through this man, a covenant of peace, and to live in this revelation of Judaism was called following The Way. Her mother had believed in this news, the Good Story, at once. Priscilla had followed. She loved the freedom the believers called "grace." She was free from sacrifices, from rituals, from hundreds and hundreds of rules, most of which she broke unintentionally and often before she even left the house in the morning.

But then the world unraveled. Marcellus, barely two years younger than she, came of age and joined her father in running the family business. That did not seem a reason for rejoicing, although she had never understood her misgivings. Then her mother grew weak and had to sleep in the afternoons. Tensions in the synagogue grew between Jews living under the new covenant and the Jews who lived under the first. Slowly, every source of comfort and security was lost.

Her thoughts flitted to Aquila. He followed The Way. Her mother shared many conversations with Aquila about faith, especially as her strength waned. Roman law made certain that servants had no more rights than a chamber pot, yet at the end of Mother's life, she wanted Aquila and Priscilla both to pray for her. She wanted Aquila to speak the final words she would hear, not Marcellus.

That awful afternoon, Marcellus had slapped Aquila, and when Marcellus swung his hand back with an aim to slap Priscilla next, Aquila grabbed his wrist. Their eyes locked, but not a word was spoken. Marcellus's arm shook as Aquila remained steady. Service had made Aquila strong, stronger than Marcellus would ever be. Marcellus took a step back, and Aquila released him. Marcellus left the room and did not return that day, not even when Mother died.

Priscilla was too grief stricken to remember anything else about that day.

Aquila was just a servant, after all, and not a man any woman would pay attention to. If she had only known.